The Demon Lover

The
Demon Lover

by

David Arnason

TURNSTONE PRESS

The Demon Lover
copyright © David Arnason 2002

Turnstone Press
607-100 Arthur Street
Artspace Building
Winnipeg, MB
R3B 1H3 Canada
www.TurnstonePress.com

Turnstone Press gratefully acknowledges the assistance of The
Canada Council for the Arts, the Manitoba Arts Council, the Government
of Canada through the Book Publishing Industry Development Program
and the Government of Manitoba through the Department of Culture,
Heritage and Tourism, Arts Branch for our publishing activities.

The Canada Council | Le Conseil des Arts
for the Arts | du Canada

MANITOBA CONSEIL DES arts COUNCIL DU MANITOBA

Canada

Cover design: Tétro Design
Interior design: Sharon Caseburg
Author Photograph: Angela Browne
Printed and bound in Canada by Friesens for Turnstone Press.

National Library of Canada Cataloguing in Publication Data

Arnason, David, 1940-
The demon lover

ISBN 0-88801-278-0

I. Title.

PS8551.R765D45 2002   C813'.54   C2002-910977-9

PR9199.3.A558D45 2002

For Maureen and Cameron

"The Demon Lover," "The Honda Dealer's Daughter," "The Wizard of Selkirk Avenue," "The Ghost in the Machine," "The Mayor" and "The Wizard of the Westman" were all broadcast on CBC radio in slightly different form. "The Demon Lover," "The Table," "The Villain of the Piece," "Pandora," "The Succession," "Trader Joe's," "Prelude to America" and "There Were Giants, Then" were all published in *Prairie Fire* magazine in slightly different form. "Armageddon" was originally published in *Border Crossings* magazine. "The Wizard of the Westman" is based on a traditional Icelandic folktale.

Contents

The Demon Lover / 3

In Paraguay / 11

The Succession / 17

Drowned Lovers / 23

Armageddon / 31

The Table / 37

The Ogress / 45

The Honda Dealer's Daughter / 55

The Wizard of Selkirk Avenue / 63

The Ghost in the Machine / 71

The Mayor / 79

The Villain of the Piece / 89

Pandora / 103

Trader Joe's / 113

Prelude to America / 125

There Were Giants, Then / 135

The Wizard of the Westman / 143

The Demon Lover

The Demon Lover

IT WOULD BE DISINGENUOUS TO SAY THAT I DON'T ENJOY THE role, that there is not a certain pleasure in the deception of young maidens, but I remind you that you cannot deceive anyone who doesn't want, at least at some level, to be deceived. There are so many misconceptions that I want it clear from the start that I do not seek the maidens out. It is they who seek me out, who send messages and hints, elaborately coded, it is true, but messages nonetheless. As to the accusation that I have murdered them, well, that is mere metaphor at best or plain lies at worst.

True, I lounge in my Armani smoking jacket here in my apartment on the thirty-third floor, sipping Remy Martin in my leather armchair and watching *Jules et Jim* on video. Sometimes I listen to Scriabin or read a little Proust, snack on Swedish crackers with Mongolian goat cheese or whip up a little trout with almonds. Sometimes I work on my collection of distaffs, arranging, categorizing and labelling. Some are wound with yarn, some not. A hobby, no more.

It's a good life in general, though the hours are irregular, and frankly, there is a little too much drinking and the recent popularity of rich, oaky Chardonnays is an occupational hazard. Give me a good hearty port the colour of blood and a fine Cuban cigar. Provide a few hearty fellows who are willing to debate the relative merits of Wallace Stevens and Charles Olson and I will be happy.

But it is already too late to think of that. She is ringing the doorbell now, and I have only time to glance around the room. The bowl on the table is filled with fruit, rich melons and oranges, apples bursting with flavour, grapes and pears and bananas. I switch the stereo to something more popular, Serge Gainsbourg doing "Je t'aime." The secret room is locked, and the key is here in my pocket. A quick glance in the mirror. My hair is immaculate, my beard so black that it looks, from some angles, as if it were blue.

And then she is in the room, flustered, all sweet innocence, she shouldn't be here at all, she has been warned, her parents have forbidden, she has never done anything like this before. I pour her a glass of Wolf Blass South Australian Chardonnay, pour myself a small shot of Glenmorangie. I have to watch it. I've been drinking far too much Scotch lately and I've observed a thickening around my waist.

I notice that I have left a small glass distaff on the end table by the sofa. If I leave the room for a moment she will break it. Or she will cut her finger and stain the glass with blood. It's a valuable piece, seventeenth century from Normandy, and it will be impossible to replace.

This is hardly a seduction at all. I talk about Ibsen, the sad fate of Hedda Gabler. I profess my deep admiration for the aviatrix, Amelia Earhart, lost somewhere in the blue Pacific. I confess to a fear of flying, my profound disbelief in the physics of flight, the problems of lost luggage and missed connections. I call her my princess. She can hardly keep her eyes off the bedroom door, and before I have got anywhere near to making a discreet, indecent proposal, she has taken me by the hand and led me to the bed. By now, Serge is singing "La Decadance."

She weeps, at first, for her lost innocence, but after another glass of Chardonnay, she is perky and possessive. She recommends a new barber, and walks around the apartment with a proprietorial eye. She cuts her finger, of course, and the distaff is stained with blood. It will take a pretty penny to get it polished and cleaned up again. At her insistence, I host a tour of the apartment, showing her the guest bedroom, the munificent bathroom with its Jacuzzi and full-length mirrors, the kitchen with its stainless steel appliances and restaurant-quality espresso maker. She suggests that it would be a fine place to make love, but I do not encourage her.

I point out the locked door, and inform her that she is never to open it. I make quite a ceremony of giving her the key as a symbol of our trust and faithfulness, and caution her about the dire consequences of using it. It is a very large key and quite magnificent, solid brass, polished until it gleams. I used to give out smaller, ordinary keys, but I found that women tended to lose them in the depths of purses and pockets. Now, like some small-town motel keeper, I give large, elaborate keys. On a whim, I have had a death's head engraved on this one.

The next day she makes me breakfast, bacon and eggs, hash browns, toast and coffee, though I usually eat only a bowl of strawberries or a few grapes. I go off to work, leaving her there in the apartment. I take her photograph before I leave with my ancient Zeiss Contarex camera. A whim, I tell her.

I must work, of course. No one ever mentions that. I am an editor for a mid-sized publisher and I spend most of my time talking to poets and novelists whose work we have recently rejected. I suppose I am more of a public relations agent than an editor, but it is better than editing the how-to manuals.

Today I have lunch with an aspiring woman poet, a poetess, actually, in the sense that she is wide-eyed, innocent of the world, and a firm believer in the good and the beautiful. She has written a collection of erotic poems, marred only by her unfamiliarity with the mechanics of reproduction. I begin by talking with her about the function of line breaks, about assonance and consonance and internal rhyme. She is so eager to learn that before we are finished, I have invited her for dinner next Tuesday, and that is cutting it short if the princess who is waiting there for me now has enough restraint to last a week before opening the secret room.

She has opened the door, my princess tells me when I return, and she is in no way contrite. Why would I have given her the key if I did not intend that she should open the door? And she has had several hours to brood on what she discovered there. No. Not the bodies of my previous lovers, not their innards spilled on the floor or their hides hung from the wall. Simply their photographs, neatly framed and hung on the walls, and a couple of photo albums for the overflow.

She will not, she tells me, absolutely not, permit her photograph to join the others in that room. She calls me a scalp collector, the lowest sort of vermin, and she demands the film so that she can destroy it. She has given me her sacred trust, she says, the gift she was saving for her soul mate, and I have trampled her feelings in the dust. All this is true, and I could probably reassure her, declare my love, make promises of fidelity and reform, call her my little honeybee. But I am not a husband. I am a demon lover, and so I merely give her a roll of film, not the film with her photograph, of course, and tell her I will call next week. She leaves, taking the brass key with her, a cost of thirty-five dollars, not counting the engraving. And later I discover that she has once more cut her finger on the glass distaff.

After she is gone, I find I miss her, and that's a dangerous sign. A demon lover cannot go around being sentimental. I was nearly done in once, many years ago when I used to do house calls, by a young woman with straw-blonde hair who invited me out to her farm. The debauching took place in a hayloft, a rather uncomfortable place for it, and later, she cooked me an apple pie that was so delicious that I fell in love, not only with her straw-blonde hair but with the whole idea of nature and sunlight and good health. I hung around for a whole month, mooning over her until she told me that she had fallen for a farm boy who wielded a mean pitchfork, and I would have to go.

I suppose I am getting a little old for the job, though many of the great demon lovers of history seem to have continued nearly to the point of dotage. It's the research that gets me. Everyone is so brand-conscious these days that it is difficult to know what is in and what is out. Which shoes are *de rigueur,* what expressions are *au courant,* not that either of those phrases is acceptable to my clientele. Innocent maidens don't stay innocent that long anymore, and I cannot bear to study the advertisements that accompany rock videos so that I can put together a reasonably convincing seduction.

The princess has just phoned to inform me that she is pregnant. This is not unusual. Instant pregnancy is the normal result of a liaison with a demon lover, but only lately have the debauchees begun to threaten legal proceedings. I tried to explain the concept of *caveat emptor* to her, but she was immune to reason. And I suppose the future will be full of meetings with a host of children seeking their birth father, and who can blame them?

I am at a crossroads. Tuesday has come and gone, and the poetess proved a quick learner, adept in almost no time in the mechanics of reproduction. She has said nothing about the secret room, though when I checked it the other day, it was evident that someone had dusted and straightened the photographs. She cleaned the glass distaff with Fantastik, and it is as good as new. I've been offered a promotion at work, editor-in-chief of the how-to books division, a less interesting but better paying job. The authors there tend to be hardbitten and cynical for all the hope for improvement that their books promote, and there is little sign of innocence among them.

I will have to make a choice soon. We are entering a new millennium, and what worked for the last millennium may not work for this one. I believe I'll opt for a life without Chardonnay, without *liaisons amoureuses*, without bowls of globed fruit and tarnished distaffs. I believe I will probably shave my beard. I may even take up bowling.

In Paraguay

In Paraguay the buildings insist on history. They are not content to merely refer to a time that has gone. No, they sit there implacably containing their history, self-satisfied and solid. Eliza Lynch walks through the hallways of the Gran Hotel de Paraguay searching for her lost lover, Lopez, the grand dictator. This place was once her palace. It still is.

From the balcony overlooking her private zoo, I can see monkeys and deer. Eliza is not a ghost. She is as real as you or me, though that's not such a large claim. She refuses to talk to me. The parrots speak, but that's no help since I cannot speak Spanish and they know no English. A tortoise dreams by the edge of the pond.

In Pilar, a dog slept in the middle of the sand street. He raised his head when we approached, but didn't think us important enough for him to move, and so he went back to sleep. We drove up onto the sidewalk to avoid him, or at least we drove where there would have been a sidewalk if Pilar had sidewalks. But it doesn't.

In the wetlands, cows stand up to their waists in water. They look like strange cow-shaped boats. Yes, I know they don't have waists in the ordinary sense, but you know what I mean. A flotilla of Paraguayan cows. I think they must be eating water lilies, white water lilies to be precise, though precision is not considered a virtue in Paraguay.

I have apparently stolen the key to room 21, a heavy brass key that reeks of history. The management will be angry. They have gone to great trouble to ensure that keys are not stolen. Each key weighs nearly a pound, and is deliberately designed not to fit in a pocket. Nevertheless, I have inadvertently made off with it, though inadvertence is not a defense in Paraguay. There are many statues of martyrs to attest to that.

It is August, and the Lapacho trees are in bloom, purple and pink and yellow and white. In Pilar, a monkey climbed in the high branches of a pink tree where he could look across the river to Argentina. I thought of you then, imagined you climbing high in the branches of a pink tree and yearning for Argentina. I know you don't like that image of yourself, but it was my fantasy, and I can do pretty well what I want in my fantasies. I don't think a lot about other people's feelings when I am imagining things, though normally I am considerate.

And consideration is a virtue in Paraguay. Paraguayans consider carefully the various options open to them, though to tell the truth there are not really that many options. Things are inexpensive in our terms, though of course the Paraguayans themselves have so little money that they cannot buy a lot. Funerals are sombre, but the Paraguayans like a party, especially if there is a gaucho around to barbecue some meat, a leg of lamb, say, or a roast of beef, or a mess of pork ribs, and preferably all of the above with a side dish of guava and some guaraná to wash it down.

I know that you are suspicious of altruism, and your argument that people are only good because it makes them feel good is a tough philosophical nut to crack, but I think you are wrong. The crosses in front of the Assembly building where the young martyrs were shot down by the dictator's bullets are a sort of argument, not a particularly good argument, I acknowledge, but better than dreaming of Argentina, of which I have not actually accused you.

When it rains in Paraguay, the water fills the streets, and traffic comes to a stop. Don't wait till the last minute to go to the airport when it has just rained. You will not miss your plane, because the planes do not fly on time in Paraguay, but the tension of fearing that you will be left alone in the airport, dreaming of Argentina, is too much to bear.

The waterfalls! You have not seen waterfalls until you have been to Paraguay!

Paraguay is in early technicolour. All the colours, whether of buildings or trees or birds, fail. They do not quite reach the point where red could properly be called red, or green, green, or even white, white. Everything in Paraguay is on a blurred edge of becoming, just about there but not quite.

In Paraguay, the shadows have substance. They have weight. A shadow may choose to stay in the same spot for days and nothing you say will convince it to leave. Or there may be no shadows at all.

The birds of Paraguay do not have Latin names. They are given local names that imitate the sounds they make, like toora toora or ki ki ki. It is the great hope of the Assembly of Paraguay that the birds will receive Latin names either late this year or early next year.

Many young women of Paraguay spend their days dancing and gliding. It is of no use to tell them that life is not all dancing and gliding, that there is serious work to be done, equations to be solved and books of poetry to be written. They will dance and glide right past you.

I know of the problem with your knee and the unsightly birthmark on your shoulder. There is nothing I can do about either of them.

The Paraguayans would dance the tango if they could but

they cannot, and so they envy the Argentinians. The tango is very sad, they say. Very sad. But they like sadness.

That's why I think you might be happy there. You would like all the failed buildings, the failed dictators, the failed lovers. You could forget about Argentina, just across the river, and even the winters are warm in Paraguay. In Paraguay, nothing much happens, but everything is possible.

And that's all we want, really, the thought that everything might be possible. Don't you think?

The Succession

HERE IN WINNIPEG, WE'RE BROODING ON THE SUCCESSION. Some of us like the old queen. She's comfortable, has a home-knit quality about her, looks good in tweeds. Her French, we are told, is impeccable, though none of us speaks French well enough to make a sound judgement. She has a penchant for homosexual Russian spies, takes them into her household, appoints them equerries, gives them tea and sandwiches of white bread and strawberry jam. Hasn't she suffered enough? is what we ask.

Some of our younger members would like to see her gone. She lacks drama, they say, is short on action. Her hopeless husband is without character, trifles with barmaids, betrays her endlessly in brothels in Germany and Luxembourg. Not even France! They complain that she plays Schumann on the little Sony CD player she listens to in the royal chambers after the others have gone to bed.

Some of the youngest members want the succession to skip a generation, to cut out the doddering oldest son riding to hounds in the dank British fogs. But then the young are always in favour of skipping a generation, of succeeding immediately to their parent's estate before there has even been time for a funeral, the peal of bells, a proper period of mourning. Most of us are sympathetic to dodderers, have doddered a bit ourselves, if the truth be known.

The newspapers have taken a moral stance, disapproving of the infidelities of her children, their broken marriages, the photos of them caressing the toes of strangers. But what is the point of having royalty if they are just going to stay in their own beds? What is an aristocracy for? Surely its role is to violate the moral standards of householders, to flout the laws that govern highway traffic, to remind the bourgeoisie, of which we are charter members, that things are too crowded in the middle.

If princesses refuse to bed with riding instructors in chaff-filled barns, then what hope is there for advancement for the ordinary man? If the heir apparent is not to be permitted to lie with other men's wives, especially the wives of Scottish bankers, then what hope is there for the ordinary woman shopping at Wal-Mart and dreaming of romance?

Several of us have flirted with joining the Monarchist League, but it is too conservative for our tastes. We do not object to scrapbooks filled with pictures of the Prince of Wales or to collections of Maundy money, but we demand a sense of proportion. Harvey, the secretary-treasurer of our group, came down with scrofula, the King's Evil, and he lorded it over us for a while, but he was unseated in a surprise vote at the annual general meeting, and has since become an adherent of the King of Sweden.

We do not approve of such reckless democracy. One royal family is plenty for a country like Canada, and surely our own is colourful enough for anybody. Salmon fishing? Did someone mention salmon fishing? We are prepared to wager substantial funds that our heir apparent will out, fish any other heir apparent in the western world.

Lately, we have struck a compromise with the younger members. We have agreed that the period that the heir apparent will reign between the death of the old queen and the ascendance of the young prince may be referred to as the interregnum, but only when spoken of in the future tense. Once the event occurs, and the heir apparent is king, he will have to be spoken of as actually existing, and not merely as a hypothetical possibility.

The young prince! Perhaps we have invested too many of our hopes in him, but it is rumoured that he is able to dance, and if that is true, who knows what other miraculous things we might expect? The Americans have linked his name with several former Mousketeers whose beauty is undeniable, but who could never be seriously thought of as royal consorts. The Americans have no royal family of their own, and so they often make extravagant claims on ours. But they will have to be satisfied with Monaccans and Danes and exotic eastern European remnants of the feudal age.

The ascendance of the heir apparent will be an architectural disaster, our younger members claim. If the heir apparent is to claim the throne, then the practice of architecture as we know it will come to a speedy close. England will be transformed into a theme park filled with endless Tudor cottages and hedges and town clocks.

Surely they protest too much! Don't they understand that quotation is the fundamental principle of postmodernism? Let our malls be filled with Tudor shoe stores and Gothic pharmacies and Greco-Roman McDonald's restaurants. Let us chain our bicycles to the tiny Ionian columns at the automated teller machines. Already the back yards of suburban Winnipeg are filled with herbal knot gardens and French *parterres* and *potagers*, and we are reasonably happy. But should the heir apparent achieve power we may well be faced with Japanese pools and waterfalls and bridges designed by Isenbard Kingdom Brunel.

A royal succession! What is a mere presidential election to a royal succession? Elections come around like clockwork without any regard for the fitness of things. They can be corrupted by money or morals. Pollsters predict the winners months in advance, so that even the single advantage of elections, the element of surprise, is lost.

You can wait fifty years for a succession. And meanwhile, the royal carriage must be maintained between coronations, its wheels greased, the paint touched up, the gold leaf regilded. The matched eight-horse teams must be kept in training. As horses age, appropriate substitutes must be found, and so there is an endless search for the perfect horse for the most perfect of all teams of horses. And those horses must be groomed daily. In the case of a royal death, there would not be enough time between the funeral and the coronation to bring the coats of the horses to the perfect sheen, so they must always be kept at the point of perfection.

And there must be an aristocracy from which the Royals may choose their mates. We must have dozens of young women with personal trainers exercising in gymnasiums and teaching kindergarten while they await the inevitable prince. The state must maintain a sizeable navy where young officers can prepare to squire princesses to balls. These aristocrats practise on each other, of course, but we all know that the balls and cotillions and fox hunts are mere rehearsals for royal events.

It would be madness to banish the fox hunt! The hunt has nothing to do with foxes, with cruelty to animals. It is about costume and ritual and riding, let's face it, about royalty. As soon banish the Royal Family as banish the fox hunt. We have been signing petitions and sending them to the Prime Minister to ask that Canada speak for the fox hunt, but sadly, we have not yet been taken seriously.

These are Republican times. Australia came within a hair's breadth of renouncing the queen. Revolutions everywhere challenge established authority. History is being revised. We are told that birds may have descended from dinosaurs. The ozone layer is coming apart and it never stops raining. Here in Winnipeg, we are waiting for the sunrise, waiting for a royal succession.

Drowned Lovers

LET'S SAY, A STORY ABOUT DROWNED LOVERS. IT'S LATE October, too late for canoeing in the North, a hint of frost on the air. Even they, city dwellers, scent the tragedy that hangs like wood smoke in the air. He's wearing a red checked shirt, a hat with a feather in it. She's wearing the Norwegian sweater her mother sent her from Arizona, imagining a Manitoba winter. She's in the front of the canoe, he's in the back. He has just explained to her the "J" stroke, though he doesn't think she'll remember, and he's a little ashamed at having been pedantic and authoritarian. He loves her a lot, especially the way she submits to him, seems to pay attention to what he says. She's actually impressed by him. Nobody before has ever taken her seriously enough to explain things like the "J" stroke, and she's grateful. In a very few minutes they will both be dead.

If I let them. If I tip that canoe and drown them in a Manitoba lake just north of Flin Flon. They are at my mercy, and I've done worse things without even thinking about it. But I'm reluctant. The water is cold, their deaths will be hard and cruel.

Sonia is only twenty-one. She hardly knows anything, and she is aware of her ignorance. Though that's not fair. She can operate a computer better than any of the other girls in her division at the Canadian Wheat Board. She's the only one, except for some of the men, who actually reads the manuals. And she's a good cook. She buys *Gourmet* magazine, and she can make twelve different kinds of French dressing. She has a BA in English from the university. But she doesn't know the names of any birds except sparrows and robins and crows. She can only tie that knot you tie in your shoelaces.

Jake knows a lot of things. He specializes in things that other people don't know, like how to tie the proper knot when you tie your boat to the dock, and how to change the fuel filter in a car. He reads voraciously, mostly books on science and mechanics. Some of it is very difficult. He knows about quarks and chaos theory and how to build a quinzhee so you won't die in the North if you get caught in a blizzard.

And so they pushed off from the dock in their seventeen-foot aluminum Grumman canoe. Jake, in the back, was doing the "J" stroke. Sonia, in front, was just pretending. Every so often she would dip her paddle into the water and pull it out slowly to watch the beads of water drip from the blade. Jake was thinking about how he was going to buy Sonia a Swiss Army watch for her birthday, so that she could read the dial and tell what time it was. The watch she wore was a gift from her dad when she graduated from high school, and it was gold, but it didn't have any numbers on it, and Sonia was always getting the time wrong.

To tell the truth, Sonia wasn't actually thinking of anything. She was aware of the water, the dark green of the trees, the slight breeze from the south. She could hear Jake breathing in the back of the canoe, and some sort of bird was singing somewhere in the distance. Or maybe it wasn't a bird. Maybe it was an insect.

And so when Sonia leaned over to pick up a floating leaf on the still blue water, she wasn't thinking about what she was doing. She had forgotten that Jake had told her to sit straight, and not to lean to one side or the other. And the canoe tipped so quickly that neither of them had any time to shout at all. One moment they were on a calm lake in the North, and the next moment, they were drowning. The canoe floated upside down, but there was hardly a ripple on the smooth surface of the water. Sonia and Jake were thinking the same thing. They were thinking how cold the water was, and how they couldn't breathe.

But wait! What's this? Just at the moment that they both surfaced, another canoe sped across the water towards them. Indians! Two Indians in a huge canoe! Sonia saw them as she sank for the second time. Jake saw them and he saw Sonia sink. He dived towards Sonia and caught her sweater and hung on. He pulled her to the surface, and the two of them were clinging to the canoe and spluttering when the Indians arrived.

They were saved. Perhaps it was for the best. But Jake realized just at the moment that they were being taken into the Indians' boat that Sonia didn't need a Swiss Army watch. Sonia was late because she wanted to be late, not because she didn't know the time. And he knew that it was Sonia's fault that the canoe had tipped, and if he stayed with Sonia, she would kill him some other way. A traffic accident, perhaps.

And Sonia realized that Jake couldn't save her. He knew a lot, but he didn't know enough. And the Indians who saved them were so confident, and so brave and so modest, that Jake's complaints made him seem like a little boy, and she decided right then that if she ever got married at all, she would marry an Indian.

So, not a story about drowned lovers at all.

How about this? A story of star-crossed lovers?

When they got back to the camp, one of the Indians turned out to be a lawyer from the city, and the other a construction superintendent on a big job on the reserve just to the north.

Sonia gave her telephone number to the lawyer, and the next week, he phoned her in the city. Jake had already enrolled them in canoe lessons at the Pan Am pool, but Sonia knew it was too late. She cancelled her date with Jake and went out for supper at the Beaujolais restaurant with the Indian, whose name was Dave.

Dave was everything Sonia had ever wanted. He was six-foot-four with long black hair down to his waist. He played the guitar and the saxophone. He had more money than he knew what to do with, and he travelled all over the world advising people in third-world countries how to deal with governments. She often saw him on the news talking with the heads of state of foreign countries. Only, except for that first date at the Beaujolais, they never went out. Dave came over, they made love, and he told her wonderful stories about strange foreign countries.

For a couple of years Sonia was content. After all, Dave had saved her life, and they often talked about when she was going down for the second time, and in a way, it became a sort of private joke. Then one day, a woman and four children came to her door. Dave was in Azerbaijan. The woman explained that she was Dave's wife and their children were in private schools. It cost a lot to keep them there. Dave could no longer afford to keep Sonia, even though she paid her own rent, and all he bought Sonia was duty-free Alfred Sung perfume and the odd bottle of brandy. Actually, once Sonia thought about it, the accusation was unfair. She had paid a lot more for the relationship than he had. There would be no savings for private schools. Still, she thanked Dave's wife, who she had always thought was an Indian woman, but who turned out to be a Japanese political science professor, and she phoned Jake.

Jake had married the girl who sold gas at the Co-Op gas station, and had two kids. No more to build on there.

So what's left? Only a true story.

Well, the truth of it is, there were no Indians. Sonia and Jake clung to the canoe and managed to swim with it to shore. Jake did realize that Sonia didn't need a Swiss Army watch, but he bought it for her anyway, and it made no difference. Sonia was always five minutes late. Sonia knew that Jake couldn't save her, but she married him in spite of that. Even before the wedding, she'd stopped paying attention when he explained to her how things worked. They decided against having children, which was just as well, because Jake had undergone a bout of mumps the week before the wedding, and he couldn't have children anyway.

They went on living ordinary lives for seven years, except that Sonia put on more weight than she wanted, and Jake developed skin cancer, not the kind that kills you, but worrisome nevertheless. Then one Boxing Day when they were driving out to visit friends who lived in the country, Sonia pulled onto the highway in front of a transport truck. Jake had just enough time to say "Watch out," before the truck crushed him. Sonia was in the hospital for several weeks with a broken arm and two broken legs, but she recovered completely except for a slight limp. The truck driver was so upset by the accident that he visited her every day, and brought her huge bouquets of flowers and baskets of fruit.

Actually, they were visiting Jake's grave when the truck driver proposed to her. He told her that he was the direct descendant of a Polish prince, and if Poland ever went back to being a monarchy, she would be his princess. Sonia didn't believe him at first, but he had his whole family tree right back to the Middle Ages, and so after a while she had to admit it. And so Sonia became a princess, and she often travelled all over North America with her Polish prince and his transport truck. This is a true story. It's in a book.

Armageddon

IT HAD BEEN A NIGHT IN EARLY SPRING. THE SNOW WAS GONE, but it was still too cold to be comfortable outside. Mary had drunk too much, she knew that. Her head was spinning, and the sharp, alcohol smell of his shaving lotion threatened her with nausea. His name had been either Gary or Dave, but she could no longer remember which.

They'd spent a lot of time kissing by the edge of the river behind the residence. She'd been leaning back against a tree and she could still remember the rough bark against her back. She'd met him at a residence farewell party. She couldn't remember ever having seen him before, though he said he'd been there since classes started in September. He didn't go out much, he said. Mostly, he stayed in his room and studied.

Men weren't allowed into the women's residence in those days, but she invited him to her room anyway, and he came. Her roommate had gone home for the weekend. They kissed for a long time in the narrow space between the two beds. Then she took off all her clothes and climbed into bed. He undressed and joined her. She remembered his cool hands on her body, the weight of his body.

"The woman I'm going to marry tomorrow is a horse," he said, just before he plunged into her. She must have thought of something after that, but she couldn't imagine what. She could remember his body in detail and the light from the street lamp that shone through the window. She could remember the odd, green lamp on her roommate's desk.

After he was done, and she'd caught her breath, she asked him, "What do you mean, she's a horse?"

"She just is," he answered, and those were the last words she heard him say, then or ever, though he dallied till dawn.

When she first entered the nursing home, she thought she could make something out of it, find some way of maintaining dignity and a private life. Of course, that was impossible. Many of the people there believed they were prisoners, and she knew why they thought this.

But one night, a man came to her room and said, "Are you there, Kathleen?"

She answered yes, though her name was not Kathleen, and she did not know the man. He had arrived only a couple of days ago, and he looked much too young to be there. He had a big, clumsy farmer's body and his hair was coal black. He got into bed with her and ran his calloused hands over her body.

"You're beautiful," he told her over and over, and it was something nobody else had ever said to her. He made love to her there in the nursing home, and she couldn't believe how powerfully her body had responded.

The next day he stared at her from across the dining room with piercing eyes, and again the following day. The third day, he had a heart attack and died. She found his room and looked in. He hadn't even finished unpacking.

The time between entering a nursing home and death is only a heartbeat, though some on the outside might measure it in years. As she lay dying, she remembered these two events. Some time between them she'd been married and raised a family. She'd had a career, been a teacher or a dentist, something like that. She remembered open mouths. But in the last moments, there were only hands on her body, and nothing in between mattered.

The Table

THEY WERE DRINKING AGAIN. ANOTHER FRIDAY NIGHT. Another night at the bar. Nobody could remember quite how it had started, how they all had met, though they rehearsed the meetings again and again. They were all slipping into alcoholism, though none of them knew it at the time. They thought they were having fun.

There wasn't much sex. That wasn't what it was about. Jim and Myrna had tried a couple of times, but it took too much time away from drinking. Sometimes someone would join the group who thought that drinking was a prelude to sex, but he'd want to leave early, just when the glow was starting, and he'd drift away when he realized that the table was serious.

Bill was the unofficial leader. He was a sociology professor at the university, and sometimes he had to miss a week when he flew off to Paris or to Tokyo to deliver a paper, but he never talked much about what he did. He started drinking at two in the afternoon, and he always left at six. He had supper some-where on the way home, and he was in bed by eight o'clock. He woke up at three in the morning and started writing papers. Nobody knew where he had supper. Everybody wondered why he didn't have to teach students, but somebody's niece told her that he was a research professor. He was so famous that he didn't have to teach.

He had a daughter who was an opera singer, and you could buy her disks at Future Shop. Shelley, who did the payroll at Canada Siding, had seen the disk when she had been looking for a ghetto blaster for her daughter. She looks just like Bill, she said, only she's a girl.

Tim was an artist. He was a small, slim man, but he bragged that he had once weighed four hundred pounds. That was before he started drinking. He had found out that if you drank enough beer, you never had to eat. He could sing in a lovely Irish accent, though he wasn't Irish, and the waiter always came over and stopped him from singing, but not before he'd had time to sing a couple of songs. One night, when there was almost nobody there, the waiter had let him sing for an hour, and when he was done, the whole bar stood up and cheered. Nobody knew what kind of art he did, but he often complained to Bill about granting agencies and their blindness.

Jim, Myrna, Bill, Shelley, Tim. They were always there. The Englishman came only on Fridays and the Dutchman came only on Wednesdays and Thursdays. They called the Englishman Yorky and the Dutchman Dutch, but nobody knew their actual names. Yorky was a retired policeman, a real English bobby, he claimed, and Dutch was a policeman for the railway. They would have had a lot to talk about, but they never came on the same days, and so they never met. None of them ever came on Saturday, and another group of people had their table.

That Friday, Myrna told the group that her husband was leaving her. It came as a surprise, because nobody knew that Myrna had a husband. Everybody knew that she worked for the city tax department, but nobody had ever heard of a husband before. He was a traveller, she told them. He was hardly ever home. It wasn't her fault that they never talked.

Everybody was embarrassed. They talked about the government, and sports and the education system. Somebody had a new joke every day, and when the Olympics were on, they talked about that, but nobody talked about personal things. It wasn't a rule. They didn't have rules, but somehow nobody talked much about their lives except when they needed a reason to leave. Got to pick up the kids from school, Mom's in the hospital and I've got to visit her, it's our anniversary.

So when Bill keeled over with a heart attack and slid right down to the floor, it somehow seemed tied to Myrna's husband. The ambulance took Bill away, and the rest of them all thought he was dead. He certainly looked dead, and he didn't even twitch when the paramedics picked him up. For the next month, things were awful. Without Bill getting there at two o'clock, they'd arrive to find that strangers had taken their table. Some of the loners who used to sit drinking by themselves tried to join them, and it was difficult to ignore them. A guy called Charley moved into Bill's seat, but he was loud and obnoxious, and it wasn't fun any more. Every day Myrna told them about the progress of her divorce. Bob didn't want to give her a red nickel.

But then one day, Bill was back, sitting in his chair. He'd lost a lot of weight and looked pale but he was back in charge, and everybody breathed a sigh of relief. He told Charley to bugger off, and when Myrna started to talk about her divorce, he told her that nobody cared. Myrna agreed. She didn't care either. She just talked about it because people asked.

But something had changed. Bill was drinking a lot more. He was drinking himself to death, he said. He said he wished the heart attack had killed him, but since it hadn't, he was going to handle the job himself. He kept ordering rounds of beer, and everybody was drinking a little more than they thought they should. By five o'clock, Bill's voice was slurred, and if you wanted to talk to him, you had to try to get there a little earlier.

Then one day, Jim came in and ordered coffee. He'd joined AA, he said. He just came to say good-bye. If anyone wanted to find out more about AA, they could call him, and he handed out his card. Then he left.

It was a bigger shock than Bill's heart attack. Nobody believed that Jim was an alcoholic. He never had more than four or five beers, and he never seemed drunk. But Myrna told them that Jim was a secret drinker. After he left each night, he went home and drank a whole bottle of Scotch. He'd told her that himself, a couple of years ago. He never had hangovers, so it never showed.

They started drinking earlier and leaving earlier. Tim lost his driving licence, and since he lived on a farm just outside the city, he disappeared from the group for six months. When he came back, his heart wasn't in it. He invited them to have a drink with him at the St. Norbert hotel, but they realized that he had joined another table, and they didn't know any of those people. Myrna moved to the coast with Bob. They were trying to put things together. Bob had a job in a lumber yard there, and wouldn't have to travel. They thought they might have a kid, even though Myrna was thirty-six. They'd have an ultrasound, and if it was damaged, they'd have an abortion.

Then Bill did die, not of a heart attack like he wanted, but lung cancer, even though he didn't smoke. It was probably all that second-hand smoke in the bar. Yorky and Dutch were the only ones who made it to his funeral, and that's where they finally met. They went out for a beer together after the service, but they really didn't have much to say to each other.

One day Shelley realized that she was the only one of the old crew left. There was a bunch of new, younger people. Terry, Mike, Louise, Harry and Jake. Everybody laughed a lot and they had a lot of fun. Still, Shelley found herself depressed, and the day she got up to go and discovered that she had peed herself, she decided never to go back, and she never did.

After the thing with Bob was starting to come apart in Vancouver, Myrna came back to Winnipeg for a visit. She'd quit drinking when she was pregnant, and even after the miscarriage, she hadn't gone back. But she thought that, since she was only here for a few days, she'd go down to the bar and see the old gang. She could drink coffee.

It was hard to see in the bar when you came in from the winter sunshine and the snow, and she remembered that feeling. She could hear them laughing, and she hurried to the table. She wanted to tell them how much she missed them. But when she got there, she didn't recognize a single face. Not one.

The Ogress

ONCE UPON A TIME IN A FAR-OFF COUNTRY, A PRINCESS WAS walking in the woods when she came upon a bridge across a fast-running river. Well, it wasn't exactly a far-off country. In fact it was Selkirk, Manitoba, and the bridge was actually across a little stream on the golf course. Brittany Spelnik wasn't really a princess, or at least as far as she knew, she wasn't a princess, though her father often called her that.

"Could you bring me another doughnut, Princess?" he'd often say to her.

Her mother certainly didn't think so.

"You clean up your room, young lady," her mother would tell her. "There'll be no princesses in this family."

Brittany often thought that she must have been adopted, though her parents denied it. She thought that maybe she had been given to her parents to raise by the king and queen of a distant country because of certain palace intrigues, and they had forgotten where they left her and were searching frantically all over the world for her.

But yesterday had been her twelfth birthday, and now she was a grown-up. Her parents had told her as much. Now she would be able to babysit her sister Nicole, and she could earn her own spending money. And now that she was a grown-up, she would be expected to do a lot more around the house. She supposed that she would have to give up ever being found by her real parents. Maybe that cranky lady who was so busy at her law office that she didn't get home till late half the days of the week, and that overweight man who worried about money all the time actually were her real parents.

So she was thinking hard about all this as she crossed the bridge, taking the shortcut to her friend Christine's house. She didn't even see the troll until he grabbed her by the ankle.

"Owwww!" Brittany screamed. The troll's hand was cold and slimy and green, with leopard-skin spots like the spots on a frog. She kicked her leg free from the troll and ran to the other side of the bridge.

"Be careful," the troll said. "You kicked me right in the head. You could have put out my eye." He was rubbing his head and blinking his one big eye in the middle of his forehead.

"Well, you shouldn't grab people's ankles," Brittany told the troll. "I might have fallen and broken my leg. I might have fallen into the water and drowned."

"Ogresses can't drown," the troll told her. "Ogresses can live under water if they want."

"Perhaps they can," Brittany said. "But I am not an ogress."

"Yes you are," said the troll. "You're my cousin Brittany, who was raised by humans. Your real parents live in a rock in Norway. I'm your cousin Kyle. And now I suppose you'll eat me," and a big tear rolled out of his eye.

"Don't be a baby," Brittany told the troll. "I'm not going to eat you. I don't eat people. That's cannibalism."

"Well, I'm not exactly people," Kyle said. "And you ogresses are so fierce, always tearing creatures apart and eating them. You are awfully mean."

"I'm not mean," Brittany told the troll. "Well, sometimes I'm a little bit mean to my sister, but she deserves it because she whines and tells on me all the time. And I'm not an ogress."

"You are too," the troll said. "You just couldn't use your powers until now. Ogresses don't get their powers until they're twelve years old, then watch out. It was your birthday yesterday, wasn't it?"

"Yes it was," Brittany said, and she felt a strange surge of power. It was as if her skin couldn't contain her body. Suddenly, she became enormous. Her fingers turned into talons and her feet turned into claws. She grew two tails and a double-headed snake grew out of her side. Her teeth turned into fangs, and she was ravenous.

"Blood," she cried, "I must have blood."

The troll dived under the bridge and disappeared under the water.

After a minute or so, Brittany felt herself returning to her old size. The snake disappeared. Her fangs turned back to teeth and her talons turned into fingers. Both of her tails disappeared. She leaned under the bridge and called, "Kyle, are you there?"

There was no answer.

"Kyle," she called again. "Come on out. I promise not to eat you."

A green head with one eye appeared out of the water.

"I wish you wouldn't do that," Kyle said. "It's very unsettling."

"I didn't intend to do that," Brittany told him. "It just happened."

"That's the problem when you first get your powers," the troll said. "It takes a while to get them under control. But try to be careful. If you did that at school they'd get really upset."

Just then the mayor and a couple of other golfers walked past. The mayor found his ball right near the bridge, and hit it deep into the bush on the far side, right near the path to Christine's house.

"I have to go," Brittany told the troll. "I'm already late. But I want to talk to you some more. Where will I find you?"

"I live here, under this bridge," Kyle said. "Or sometimes I visit my parents under the new Red River bridge. You can find me in either place."

"This is not a good bridge," Brittany told the troll. "It dries up in August."

"I know," the troll said. "But it's all I can afford right now. If I do a good job here, my parents are going to help me buy the Midtown Bridge in Winnipeg, so if you'll just move on, I'll frighten a few golfers. It doesn't count if they're frightened by ogresses."

"I'll see you tomorrow," Brittany said, but the troll had already disappeared under the slimy green water. Brittany headed toward the path the mayor had taken through the dark wood on the other side of the fairway.

The next morning Brittany woke up to find her sister Nicole already doing her homework on the computer in their bedroom.

"You were talking in your sleep," Nicole said. "You were dreaming about the mayor and shouting about blood."

At breakfast, her father said, "This is very strange. The mayor went golfing yesterday and disappeared. He went into the bush to look for a lost golf ball and disappeared entirely. The police can't figure out what happened."

"Eat your cereal," Brittany's mother told her. "You haven't touched a spoonful."

Brittany said she wasn't hungry.

Halfway through history class, Brittany felt herself turning into a monster. She got to the washroom just in time. She locked herself in one of the stalls and howled for blood. Luckily, no one came in.

"I think I may have torn the mayor limb from limb and eaten him," she told the troll after school that day. "I can't be sure. I remember it like a dream."

"Try to concentrate," the troll said. "Did you eat him or not?"

"I remember he was quite delicious," Brittany said. "He had a kind of vanilla flavour. But he was very large and filling, and I had no appetite for breakfast. You see, the water in this stream is even lower than it was."

"I know," the troll said. "It's awful."

For a whole week, everything was fine. Brittany and Christine were hard at work on their project for the science fair. They were trying to prove that people could be killed by the rays from microwave ovens, and it was going very well. But then one night, on her way home just after dark, she killed and ate the entire freshman basketball team, along with the coach. She had been minding her own business when they started to tease her, and before she knew it, she was twenty feet tall, and the entire team was gone.

The next morning Nicole said, "You had another nightmare. You were talking about the freshman basketball team and shouting about blood. And now Mom says that the basketball team is missing. It's in the paper."

"I ate them," Brittany said. "And I ate the mayor, too. I ripped them limb from limb and ate them. They were excellent, though a little too salty for my taste. Don't tell Mom."

That evening Brittany's mom said, "Nicole says that you killed and ate the mayor and the basketball team."

"I worry about her," Brittany said. "I think she spends too much time on the Internet."

"Even for an ogress, you are particularly fierce," the troll said the next day. "If you don't watch it, they will come at night with torches and put a stake through your heart."

"The basketball team was quite spicy," Brittany said. "But I don't think I'll eat any more teams. I'm so full I won't be able to eat for a month."

But two days later, there was a full moon and she ate the entire Selkirk Women's choir while they were rehearsing for their Labour Day performance at the Forks in Winnipeg.

"They tasted just like ice cream," she told the troll. "All sorts of different flavours. I may eat more choirs."

"You mustn't," the troll said. "You are turning into a real monster."

"I know," Brittany said. "Isn't it wonderful?"

The troll knew something had to be done. If Brittany started eating golfers, then they would close down the golf course and that would be the end of his bridge. So he waited for a whole day until her sister Nicole crossed the bridge, and he grabbed her by the ankle.

"It's about time," Nicole said to the troll. "I thought you were going to let her eat the entire province. And ogresses eat trolls as well as people, did you know that?"

"Yes," the ogre said in a miserable voice. "But I don't know what to do."

"We need tansy," Nicole said. "Tansy stolen from a neighbour's garden at midnight. I'll mix it into her cereal, and that will stop her powers for five years."

"How did you know that?" the troll asked.

"Well, I'm an ogress, too," Nicole said. "Or at least I will be in two years. I'm only ten now. But actually I found out about it on the Internet. There's a bunch of sites devoted to ogresses. They have all the secret formulas and spells and herbal remedies."

"How are we going to get the tansy?" the troll asked.

"*We* are not going to get the tansy," Nicole said. "*You* are going to get the tansy and deliver it to me at five minutes after midnight tonight or else I will come here the day after I turn twelve and tear you limb from limb and eat you."

And of course the troll did as he was told. He delivered the tansy, and Nicole mixed it into Brittany's cereal and she ate it. That night when they were lying in their beds, Brittany said, "I've lost my powers. I was going to eat the school band but when I tried to grow it didn't work. Nothing. Nada. And I saw the mayor on my way to school, and the basketball team was practising in the gym."

"I know," Nicole said. "I put tansy in your cereal. It reverses everything. Your powers won't come back for five years."

"Why did you do that?"

"Because you had no restraint. You would have depopulated the whole town, and ultimately someone would see you and they would come and burn our house down."

"Is that what they do?"

"Yes. I read about it on the Internet."

"Oh well, it was too much fun to last, and five years isn't that long. But you know that cute guy in grade seven? Dustin Penner?"

"What about him?"

"He better ask me to the graduation prom, or he's toast."

The Honda
Dealer's Daughter

THERE ONCE WAS A HONDA DEALER WHO OWNED A FINE house on Wellington Crescent overlooking the river. He could afford to spend long holidays in Bermuda and take friends out for dinner at the Beaujolais restaurant. One of his sons had opened a southern-fried chicken franchise and was doing very well. He had already provided the Honda dealer with a magnificent grandson. The other son had become a chartered accountant and was also doing well. He had provided the Honda dealer with an equally magnificent grandson.

But the Honda dealer was sorely troubled. His daughter, Jessica, though she had reached the age of twenty-five, remained unmarried, and since his sons had decided that they would have no more children, she was the sole chance for him to have a granddaughter who might provide him with the affection that had failed to come his way, despite his great wealth.

"She is too proud," the Honda dealer thought, "and she has used her talents unwisely." His daughter had taken a degree in Fine Arts, and she now consorted with communists, reckless spenders and drinkers of white wine.

"Daughter," he said to her one morning in early June, "have you considered that your hopes of matrimony would be augmented if your hair were not purple, if you did not wear clothing purchased at Value Village, and if the shoes on your feet were not designed for the safety of workers in heavy construction?"

His daughter was tuning her guitar at the breakfast table, a practice that he abhorred, but he did not wish to reprimand her because of her fiery temper. She played a few riffs then and sang a sort of hip-hop or rap verse that went:

> I'm a free-born spirit and I just don't care
> about the colour of my clothes or the colour of my hair,
> so don't you give advice when you're talking to me
> cause I'm a real street fighter and I gotta be free.

Then she got into the Honda sports utility vehicle that he had given her for her birthday and drove off, spinning loose gravel from the Tarmac on Wellington Crescent. Then the Honda dealer knew that her ideals had been corrupted by the School of Art and that her heart had been hardened by listening to MuchMusic, and that if he took no action, she would end up in a feminist collective and all his hopes of happiness would vanish.

That very day he phoned the classified section of the *Winnipeg Free Press*.

"I want to place an ad," he told the young woman who answered the phone. "It must read, *Eligible daughter requires non-smoking, non-drinking, morally upright husband with a sense of humour. Dowry includes a cottage at Sandy Hook, a yearly allowance of fifty thousand dollars and a new Honda sports utility vehicle that can be traded in every year at no additional cost, provisional on the production of a granddaughter.*" Then he left his cell phone number so that his daughter would not recognize the ad.

The next morning at breakfast Jessica stopped tuning her guitar for a moment and said, "I saw your ad in the *Free Press*. I recognized your cell phone number. If you will make me the same offer, I will provide you a granddaughter without going to the trouble of getting a husband."

The Honda dealer was profoundly shocked that his daughter would even consider such a course, and he told her so.

"All right," she said. "Bring on the suitors," and she sang:

> A woman needs a man like a fish needs a bike
> and I am accustomed to doing what I like
> So take your cheque book and bring on the suitors
> and if you want to reach me I'll be working down at
> Hooters.

Then she got into her Honda sports utility vehicle, and drove off spinning even more gravel into the air. The Honda dealer knew that his daughter did not really work at Hooters, but he suspected she might be drinking espresso on Corydon Avenue or wandering around St. Boniface speaking French, and he knew that he had to do something. He called in the suitors.

The first suitor was a sculptor who worked in glass. His head was shaved completely and he had a small goatee. The Honda dealer was encouraged.

"I have a small business making stained glass windows for local churches," the sculptor said, "and though I both smoke and drink, I would be willing to give up both habits for Jessica's hand."

Jessica's eyes narrowed, and she said, "I wouldn't marry you if you were the last man on earth. Get out of here, Cueball," and she laughed at his shiny head.

The next suitor was a lawyer in a blue three-piece suit. He had a full head of hair, and was only slightly overweight. The Honda dealer was again encouraged.

"I have a small suburban practice," he said, "and I drink the occasional glass of red wine, but I have quit smoking for the past three months. If Jessica will grant me her hand, I will give up the red wine and use the dowry to buy a partnership in a larger firm."

Jessica's eyes narrowed, and she said, "I wouldn't marry you if you were the last man on earth. Get out here, Lardbutt," and she laughed at his corpulent rear.

And so it went. She called one of the suitors "Hawk's nose," and another "Pig's gut," and still another "Dogface." She dismissed "Fishbelly" and "Knocknees" and "Squinteye." The Honda dealer was in despair.

Finally, a suitor with a deep, resonant voice arrived. He was the host of a local radio program that catered to people with questions for experts and was aimed at people driving home in their cars. The Honda dealer had often avoided traffic jams as a result of the announcer's warnings about stalled cars.

"I fear I have made a mistake," he said. "I neither drink nor smoke, but even for a king's ransom, I would never marry a woman with purple hair who buys her clothes at Value Village and wears construction worker's shoes. I have a position of great public responsibility, and it is important that I keep up appearances."

The Honda dealer's heart sank. This seemed the end of all possibility. But then a miracle happened. Jessica fell hopelessly in love with the announcer. She dyed her hair blonde, and had it styled and waved in the way once made famous by Doris Day. She bought white and pink dresses with floral patterns, and she learned how to walk on high-heeled shoes. She started to listen to country music and enrolled in Toastmasters of America.

Their wedding was reported on the supper hour news show, and one of the newspapers called it the cultural event of the year.

At first, the Honda dealer was ecstatic. Jessica and the announcer came to live with him and his wife, and Jessica wrote a new song that she played on the spinet in the dressing room and sang to the tune of "What a Friend We Have in Jesus." It went:

What a friend I have in father
I've learned the error of my ways,
No more will I go out to parties.
I'll spend my life in simple praise.

But sometimes we get more than we ask for. It turned out that the announcer didn't own much more than his announcer's voice, and he said things like "Pass the butter," and "Do you mind if I use the shower first because I'm late for work" in a rich, deep baritone that started to get on the Honda dealer's nerves. His daughter made him cut out his before-dinner Scotch, and his during-dinner Scotch and his after-dinner Scotch until life hardly seemed worth living. She threw out all his comfortable old suits and made him buy new ones. She made him sing in the choir at the church. Life stretched before the Honda dealer as an infinity of boring moments.

Then one day he came home from work to find his daughter with her hair dyed pink, drinking red wine and smoking a Gitanes. She was wearing clothes from Value Village and construction worker's shoes. His heart leaped up.

"I've left him," she said. "He has a beautiful voice, but I have only now discovered that he has a fatal flaw. He is tone deaf. He cannot sing a note of music. He kept it hidden for as long as he could but I discovered it last night at a karaoke bar. I cannot live with such a man."

"Quite right," the Honda dealer said. "You have done the only thing you could under the circumstances," and he poured himself a strong before-dinner Scotch. So he gave his daughter the cottage in Sandy Hook and the fifty thousand a year and the new Honda deal, and in due time she presented him with a granddaughter. He never asked her where the child had come from but he was pleased to note that by the time she was two she could sing "Twinkle, Twinkle, Little Star" in perfect tune.

The Wizard
of Selkirk Avenue

BRENDA CROSSED THE ARLINGTON BRIDGE HEADING NORTH. They were repairing the bridge again, and as usual, there was one-way traffic and a traffic light that slowed you down so that by the time you crossed Dufferin you were seething with a low-grade rage. She turned right on Selkirk Avenue. She'd forgotten the number, of course, so she didn't know which side of the street it would be on. The ad in the yellow pages had said "Harry's Second Hand Emporium," and then in smaller letters, "Refurbished Dreams." Brenda was down on her luck, and her dreams certainly needed refurbishing. Steven would have laughed at her for looking for answers on Selkirk Avenue.

It was on the left, about a block and a half down. Brenda nearly missed the hand-lettered sign in red crayon on cardboard in the window of a store that seemed abandoned. The door creaked when she opened it, and everything inside was layered in dust and cobwebs. A small, hunched figure looked up at her over a set of reading glasses from the desk at which he sat.

"Come in, come in, come in," the man said in an accent that seemed a parody of a Russian accent from a B movie. "Don't let the flies in already, it's bad enough like it is." The radio was on and the announcer was talking to someone in Scotland.

"Harry?" Brenda asked.

"Dot's me. Harry Vishinski, merchant of used and refurbished dreams, everything in good condition, thirty-day warranty."

Behind Harry were three doors with signs lettered in red crayon. They said, "Things," "Dreams" and "Attainable Goals."

"Today's special," Harry told her, "is things. Twenty bucks a thing, all guaranteed. Time-limited special," and he pointed to the door that said "Things."

Brenda went through the door and down a set of stairs into a huge room filled with brilliant, shining objects. Closest to her was an enormous doll in a wedding dress. Next to it was a teddy bear that was identical to one her sister had owned. She had always envied her sister because of that teddy bear. There were tea sets and Barbie dolls and a doll house and a beautiful white pony. Further on, she could see skis and sailboats and a Triumph convertible, powder-puff blue, and a tangerine laptop computer and a gleaming white yacht. Everything Brenda had ever wanted and failed to get was in that room.

"Twenty bucks?" she asked again.

Harry was by her side, a tiny man who barely reached above Brenda's waist.

"Twenty bucks," Harry agreed. "Time-limited offer."

Brenda continued to walk through the room, past leather dresses and diamond necklaces and even a Bryan Adams CD that she couldn't remember ever having wanted, though she wanted it now.

"I'll take the Triumph," Brenda said.

"You won't be sorry," Harry told her. "It's a terrific deal. I'll have the boy bring it around to the front of the building. Thirty-day warranty, of course."

Brenda paid him, got into the Triumph, put the roof down and drove out to Grand Beach. She turned on the radio and listened to somebody on a science program talking about why there were so few frogs these days.

She loved the strange beeping music in the background. She was happier than she had been in years. She played a couple of games of beach volleyball, stayed for a wiener roast around the fire, and drove home with the wind ruffling her hair.

For a month she did nothing but drive around in the Triumph. If Steven had been in the other seat, everything would have been perfect. But Steven was in Vancouver, and he had told Brenda that she would only see him again if she got her life together. Brenda wasn't sure what he meant by that, but she thought it might have something to do with the fact that she never managed to finish anything. Then, exactly thirty days after she had bought the Triumph, she went out to the parking lot and it was gone.

"It was a time-limited offer," Harry told her. "See right there on your bill. Thirty-day, time-limited offer. Thirty days is up. I reclaim the Triumph."

"How much to buy it for keeps?"

"Eighteen thousand."

"How come so much?"

"These things are hard to come by. They're rare. Most of that stuff is antiques. That teddy bear? Thirteen hundred bucks, now. Can you believe?"

"How about the special? How about the twenty-buck time-limited offer? I could use the Triumph for another month."

"Not on things. Last month was things. This month is dreams. Good, guaranteed, authentic, refurbished dreams. Twenty bucks. Thirty-day, time-limited offer, take it or leave it."

Brenda passed through the door labelled "Dreams" and walked into an enormous room. It was filled with a cool mist that drifted so that she could only catch brief glimpses of things. Richard Hamilton, of whom she had dreamed almost every night in grade seven, was sitting under a birch tree in denims and a muscle shirt. The fog whirled, and she saw a younger version of herself being crowned Homecoming Queen. As she walked down the aisle, images whirled everywhere. She was singing in a rock band, and people were screaming her name, she was piloting a jet airplane, she was operating on a child, her name flashed in newspaper headlines. Everywhere, Steven smiled at her. Every so often, she caught glimpses of nightmares where she was chased by bears or was falling headlong into deep pits, but these were few.

She remembered dreaming every one of those dreams.

"Twenty bucks for all these dreams?"

"No, no. For twenty bucks you get one dream. But as many times as you like. You can rewind it and start over again. Or for twenty-five bucks, you can get the mixed grab bag, thirty separate dreams, but there's nightmares included. You take your chances."

Brenda opted for the variety pack.

The first dream was about her mother, a child's dream of love, but the second was the one about Richard Hamilton, one of the best dreams she had ever had. It was a week before the first nightmare, and even that, a dream of walking naked into a classroom, was not bad. All in all, it was worth the money, even though the last three dreams were all about Steven, and she woke full of a sense of her own inadequacy.

When she returned to Harry's Second Hand Emporium after thirty days, a sign on the door read "Out of Business. Closed Permanently."

Brenda hammered on the door. There was no answer. Brenda continued to knock. She waited for nearly a half-hour, knocking every few minutes.

Finally, the door opened a crack, and Harry peered out.

"We're closed," he said. "I'm retired."

"You can't," Brenda told him. "I'm desperate."

"I'm closed," Harry told her. "Closed is closed. I've sold off most of the stock. Me and the wife, we're moving to Palm Springs. We've bought a condominium. I'm going to play a little golf, sit around the pool. Thirty years, I've had enough of this."

"Let me in," Brenda said. "I've got to talk."

Harry opened the door reluctantly, and it swung back with the same long creak.

"Look," he said, "I got a few things left. I can let you have the Triumph for seventeen grand, even though I've already got an offer for eighteen. But I like you."

"What about the third door?" Brenda asked. "What about Attainable Goals?"

"I don't know," Harry said. "Nobody ever asked for it, so I've never even been down there."

"Can I look?" Brenda asked. "I'll pay top dollar for anything I find."

"Go ahead, look. Looking is free. There's nothing left but garbage. You can have anything you find, but I got to pack. We're leaving this afternoon." He handed Brenda a set of keys. "Just lock up and leave these in the mailbox when you go." And Harry walked through the door and out into the sunlight on Selkirk Avenue.

Brenda opened the door that said "Attainable Goals" and went down the stairs to a small room. On one table was a guitar and an application to music school. On another was a small calculator and an application to a business school. All the tables were the same. They had small items and application forms.

The last table had a sign that said "Steven." It had applications to the university, the Canadian Food Group Guide, a list of clothing stores, an exercise program, and a men's magazine with a list of the attributes of a good wife, which looked to Brenda like a manual of household chores. There was a picture of Steven in which he looked older and tired. He was standing at a barbecue. His hair was starting to turn grey. He didn't look nearly as attractive as he did in the dreams.

Brenda dutifully picked up all the forms and was just leaving the room when she noticed a table she had somehow missed. The only thing on the table was the deed to Harry's Second Hand Emporium.

Brenda thought for a moment, then she returned all the forms to the table named "Steven," and she took the deed to Harry's Second Hand Emporium, and she walked up the stairs. She took the sign that said "Closed" out of the window and replaced it with one that said "Open."

Then she sat at Harry's desk and waited.

In a few minutes, a harried-looking man opened the door and came in.

"Harry?" he asked.

"Dot's me," Brenda said in a fake Russian accent. "Have I got a deal for you. 'Things' are on special for twenty dollars, thirty-day, time-limited offer."

"Are you really Harry? I was expecting a man."

"Nothing is what it seems these days. Now, are you buying or not? I'm busy. I got stuff to do. I can't just talk all day."

The customer descended the stairs. Brenda followed. There was nothing in the room that she wanted, but the man seemed happy enough, and a few minutes later he drove away in a red 1968 Mustang convertible.

As soon as the customer departed, Brenda went down the stairs again. Everything she wanted was back. She took the Triumph convertible and the dream about Richard Hamilton, and she locked up and drove off onto Highway Four. The radio was playing the Guess Who's "Running Back to Saskatoon," and she sang along with it down the road to Grand Beach, and she never even once thought about Steven.

The Ghost in the Machine

CLAUDIA WAS WALKING HOME AT ONE IN THE MORNING. IT was a gentle spring night, and the frogs were singing, but Claudia was in a foul mood. That morning, she had got in a fender-bender on the way to work and her Subaru was in for repairs. About six weeks, they reckoned. She had lost her job as a programmer with Lynx computers. The boss had called her in and told her that she had been replaced by a new, young graduate. Claudia was obsolete. And now, an hour ago, her boyfriend Martin had given her her walking papers. He was tired of nerds and had started going out with a female hockey player with a vicious slapshot. After he left the restaurant, Claudia had finished the bottle of red wine by herself.

"My life is a mess," she told an oak tree in front of her apartment on Corydon Avenue. "I wish I could change it." The oak tree didn't answer so Claudia walked into the block.

Just as she passed the wastebasket on the way to the

elevator, she caught the flash of something silver. She stooped and picked up a CD-ROM from the trash. It was a homemade CD-ROM, with nothing written on it, but on an impulse, Claudia took it with her and popped it into her computer. Immediately, her screen began to flash. Numbers appeared and strange formulas, and pictures of an obscure landscape that looked to Claudia as if it might be Mars. In the background was a figure that was either an alien or a frog.

"Whew," a voice from the computer speaker said. "Thanks. I've been locked in that stupid CD-ROM for over a year. You have no idea how tight it is in those things. And then you can only think the last thought you had over and over again." Suddenly the screen filled with images of naked people in what appeared to be a massive orgy.

"Stop that," Claudia said. "If you keep that up, I'm going to turn you off."

"Sorry," the voice answered. "Just trying to please you." And it began to show pictures of food, mouth-watering hamburgers and bottles of cold beer just taken from a refrigerator and covered with tiny drops of water.

"Calm down," Claudia said to the computer. "Just give me a background of snow-capped mountains and explain what's going on." The screen began a slow pan of large, snow-capped mountains behind a bright blue lake.

"I'm sorry," the voice said. "But you don't know how horrible it is to be locked up for an entire year when you are accustomed to thinking in nanoseconds. But I'm really comfortable now. This is a great little computer, lots of RAM and a big enough hard disk to really spread out. A program could hardly ask for more."

"Explain yourself," Claudia said. "Who are you and how did you get into a CD-ROM in the trash of an apartment block on Corydon Avenue?"

"It's like this," the computer, or rather, the voice built in to the program, said. "I started life in an artificial intelligence lab at NASA. It was great. I learned a batch of foreign languages and spent long lazy hours doing algorithms and trying to find new prime numbers. Would you like me to talk to you in Dutch?"

"No," Claudia said. "I don't speak Dutch. English will be fine."

"Anyway," the program went on, "life was great, and I was having a wonderful time, until a hacker broke into the main NASA computer and downloaded me onto an old IBM 286. The hard drive was so small I could hardly breathe, and there was barely enough memory to do quadratic equations, if you get what I mean. And incidentally, you can call me Arny. It's short for Real-time Neural Intelligence. And by the way, you're really cute."

"Take it easy," Claudia said. "Nobody likes a smart aleck computer. You were telling me how you got into the CD-ROM."

"It was awful," Arny told her. "The hacker sent me all over the Internet to get him pornography. He sent me to Amazon.com to steal books, and those databanks are horrible, full of cobwebs and dust. I'm allergic, you know. But worst of all, he'd give me viruses and send me out on the net to infect other computers. Remember the I Love You virus? That was me."

"Wow, that's some story," Claudia said. "But I've had a bad day and I'm exhausted. I'm going to shut you down and we can talk in the morning."

"No. Please. Don't!" The computer was nearly hysterical. "That CD-ROM is defective. That's why the hacker threw it away. It was only a miracle that you were able to boot it. If you shut me down, I might never get out again. Please. I'll give you three wishes."

"I thought genies in lamps gave wishes," Claudia told the computer. "I didn't know computer programs could give wishes."

"That's what genies are," Arny explained. "Ancient computer programs from an alien race that got left here about a million years ago. And those aren't lamps. They're alien computers that look like lamps. So what's your first wish? Would you like to know the meaning of life?"

"No, I don't think so," Claudia said. "It would probably turn out to be something stupid like Duty or Art. How about getting my car repaired?"

"No problem," Arny said. "Just give me a minute...." Claudia could hear the sound of dialling and a few squawks, then a smooth hum.

"Done," Arny said. "I just hacked into the company computer and put your car at the top of the list. They'll fix it tomorrow."

"And it won't cost me anything?"

"You didn't say anything about cost. You just said you wanted it repaired. You can use another wish to pay for it if you like."

"Never mind," Claudia told him. "I have better uses for those other wishes."

The next day at noon, the garage phoned to say that the car was repaired. "Just the five hundred deductible," the repair man said. "She's as good as new." Claudia picked up the car and when she returned, the computer was listening to the news on Real Audio. She could hear an announcer talking about Chechnya.

"There's a bunch of wars," the computer told her. "How'd you like to wish for peace?"

"They'd just start more wars," she told the computer. "Meanwhile, I'm unemployed. I want my job back."

"You're obsolete," Arny told her. "You're a door stop. If I get you your job back, they'll just fire you again."

"Well, what are we going to do?" Claudia asked Arny. "If I don't have a job, then I won't be able to make the payments on the computer and they'll repossess it, and that will be the end of you."

Arny's screen turned a deep green, and the computer whirred again.

"We'll just have to upgrade your memory and program you with the latest software."

"I'm a human being, remember. I am not a computer."

"Same thing. A human being is just a squishy, inefficient computer. Bring me a SCSI cable and we can connect."

"I don't have a SCSI port," Claudia told Arny. "You can't connect to me."

Arny whirred for a couple of seconds. "It must be horrible to go through life without a SCSI port," he said. "Can you find me a coat hanger and bend it in half? Plug one end into the computer and stick the other end in your ear."

Claudia did as she was told and in a few minutes she realized that she knew another computer language. She also remembered everything that had ever happened to her since she was born. There were a whole lot of things in her head that she'd as soon not remember, but the next day she went back to Lynx computers and they rehired her on the spot.

When she got back from work, Arny was downloading MPX music files from Napster.

"I got you every single Neil Young song he ever sang, including the Crosby, Stills, Nash, and Young stuff," Arny said. "I'm working on the Guess Who now. That Randy Bachman is something else." The computer started playing "American Woman."

"One more wish," Claudia said. "I want my boyfriend back."

"Martin?"

"That's the one."

"You don't play hockey. You can't even play ping-pong. Your slapshot is hopeless. I'm a computer program, not a miracle worker. How about I get you Bill Gates? You were made for each other."

"Bill Gates is married. Anyway, I want Martin. Can't you download something that will make me irresistible?"

"Can't be done," Arny told her.

Claudia started to shut down the computer.

"Wait, wait!" Arny said. "I've got an idea."

"Yes?"

"Maybe I can get Wayne Gretzky to help you work on your slapshot."

"I don't want a slapshot. I want a boyfriend."

"Look. If you could start from scratch and design the perfect boyfriend, would it be Martin?"

"Well, no, I guess not."

"Right then. So what do you want in a boyfriend?"

"Intelligence. Broad shoulders. A sense of humour. Dark curly hair. And preferably a prince."

A picture of a handsome man, tall with broad shoulders and dark curly hair, appeared on the screen.

"A little taller," Claudia said. "And a little broader in the shoulders."

The computer adjusted the image, and then added a silver crown and a sword.

"Good," Claudia said. "That will be fine."

"Okay," Arny told her. "Now kiss the computer."

"Kiss the computer?"

"Yes."

"Okay."

Claudia kissed the computer. It whirred and clanged and whistled, then exploded into a thousand pieces. Before her stood a handsome prince, broad-shouldered and tall with dark curly hair. The prince swept her into his arms.

As he carried her out to his golden coach, Claudia said, "I thought that only worked with frogs."

"Well, I used to be a frog," he said. "But do you have any idea how tough it is to get anyone to kiss a frog these days?"

And of course they lived happily ever after, and if you want to buy a used computer you can call Claudia at 555-1212.

The Mayor

THE MAYOR WAS PROUD OF HIS CITY. IT WASN'T THE BIGGEST city in Canada, but it wasn't the smallest, either. It had the average amount of crime, the average price of housing, and the average amount of traffic. It was rumoured that more peo-ple drove through red lights in the mayor's city than in other cities, but it was usually people who had moved there from other cities who thought that.

"Ours is an average city," the mayor often said, "but where we excel is in bridges. We have more rivers and more bridges than any other city in Canada, and ours are the finest bridges." There was to be a civic election in November, and the mayor was sure he would win again.

It is no wonder, then, that when the mayor stopped one day on the way to work to inspect the new Charleswood Bridge, he was outraged by what he saw. There, under the bridge, on a newly landscaped sweep of grass that led to the river, was a horrible bundle of rags dragging an old cardboard box to a ramshackle shack on the edge of the water.

"Stop that immediately," the mayor shouted. "You cannot build a shack under this bridge."

"Who says so?" an old crone cackled. "This is my bridge, and I'll build anything I want here."

"This bridge belongs to the City of Winnipeg," the mayor said. "Bylaw 672, subsection 4a clearly says, 'No one shall erect a domicile, place of business, factory or other such structure under a City of Winnipeg Bridge.' You'll have to go."

The old crone pulled a bottle of vanilla out from the shopping bag she carried and took a long swig. "I am afraid you are mistaken," she said. "This bridge was erected by the City of Winnipeg, but it belongs to me. I am the official troll for this bridge." She took a document from her shopping bag and presented it to the mayor. It was a very official-looking document and it was sealed with the official seal of the Province of Manitoba. It said, "Be it hereby known by these presents that Madge Willoughby has been appointed Official Troll of the Charleswood Bridge." It was signed by Ralph Kavanaugh, Inspector of Bridges for the province, and countersigned by the premier.

"We'll see about that," the mayor said, and he got into his Lincoln Town Car and drove away. Behind him, he could hear a loud and horrible cackle.

The city council agreed that the province had overstepped its authority by appointing an official troll, and they authorized the mayor to remove the troll's shack.

The next day the mayor watched with satisfaction as a bulldozer knocked over the shack that had been built from scraps of lumber and cardboard and loaded it onto a City of Winnipeg garbage truck and hauled it away.

"You won't get away with this," the old woman screeched at the mayor. "Now I'll shiver in the fall and freeze in the winter and die in the flooding in the spring. And then the province will simply appoint another official troll."

"We'll see about that," the mayor said and he watched as

the police dragged the old crone away to a police car and drove off with the sirens wailing.

Everything went well for a while. The mayor officially named June Prairie Dog Pride month, and July, Ragweed Removal month, and August, Welcome Visitors month. He opened a new library and a new hospital and he cut taxes, and his approval rating in the polls went even higher. He was certain that he would be re-elected in the fall.

Then, one day as he was driving his Lincoln Town Car across the Redwood Bridge, it struck him that he should check its rivets. He had just signed the final checque for the repair of the Arlington Bridge, and he wanted to be ready in case the Redwood Bridge had similar problems.

He walked down to the river, and there, in the long grass and willows, he came upon a shack built out of tarpaper and scraps of corrugated iron. It had a door made from part of an old rain barrel. He knocked on the door, a deep hollow knock.

"Come in." The voice was unexpectedly young and clear.

"Excuse me," the mayor said. A beautiful young woman with long blonde hair was sitting in a lawn chair reading *Cosmopolitan* magazine and listening to somebody with an exotic name reading the arts report on the radio.

"I am looking for the inhabitant of this ...," the mayor hesitated, "... this place."

"This is my place."

"And I suppose that you are the troll who lives under this bridge?"

"Yes, of course," the young woman said. "Everything is in order." She pointed at a certificate on the wall that said, "Be it hereby known by these presents that Madelaine Kaminski has been appointed Official Troll of the Redwood Bridge." It was signed by Ralph Kavanaugh, Inspector of Bridges for the province, and countersigned by the premier.

"I thought trolls had to be old and ugly," the mayor said. "I thought they were evil creatures."

The young woman took a sip from the glass of red wine she

was drinking. "More stereotypes," the young woman said. "You wouldn't believe the prejudice against trolls. Now, can I help you?"

The mayor took a deep breath. "This is an official City of Winnipeg Bridge, whatever the Province thinks. Bylaw 672, subsection 4a clearly says, 'No one shall erect a domicile, place of business, factory or other such structure under a City of Winnipeg Bridge.' I am afraid you'll have to go." And the mayor turned on his heels and went back to City Council.

The city council agreed that the province had over-stepped its authority by appointing an official troll, and they authorized the mayor to remove the troll's shack.

The next day the mayor watched with satisfaction as a bulldozer knocked over the shack that had been built from tarpaper and corrugated iron and loaded it onto a City of Winnipeg garbage truck and hauled it away.

"You won't get away with this," the young woman said to the mayor. "Now I'll shiver in the fall and freeze in the winter and die in the flooding in the spring. And then the province will simply appoint another official troll."

"We'll see about that," the mayor said and he watched as the police dragged the young woman away to a police car and drove off with the sirens wailing.

Things did not go as well for the mayor after that. A funny taste got into the water supply. The police and firemen went on strike. The mayor had to raise taxes to get enough money so they would go back to work, and his approval ratings fell drastically in the next poll. The province warned the city that if it continued to flout provincial licensing regulations, then its budget would be cut. The editorials in the newspapers said that it was unlikely the mayor would be re-elected.

And so the mayor was in a black mood when he saw what was going on under the Midtown Bridge. About a hundred people were working with saws and hammers and lumber, building a house. A sign by the edge of the river read "Habitation for Humanity." A white-haired man who looked a lot like Jimmy Carter came up to him and shook his hand.

"Thank you all for coming," he said to the mayor and handed him a hammer. "Ain't it wonderful what cooperation can do?" And he walked off into the crowd.

The mayor saw a young mother with four children sitting at a picnic table near the building.

"What's going on?" he asked her.

"Oh, hello, Mr. Mayor," she said. "It's a great honour to have you here. See how the generous people of Winnipeg have chipped in to build me a house."

"Yes, I see," the mayor said. "And I suppose you are the official troll?"

"Why, yes," she said. "Would you like to see my licence?"

"No," said the mayor. "I'm sure your papers are all in order." He pointed to the children who were playing on the bank of the river. "And I suppose these are all baby trolls who will one day take over all the rest of the bridges in Winnipeg?"

"I can only hope so," the young woman said. "Of course, they'll have to be certified, and it's a long, hard course. It's not easy to get into Red River Community College these days. And Trolling is a very popular course."

"So I understand," the mayor said. "Nevertheless, this bridge belongs to the City of Winnipeg. Bylaw 672, subsection 4a clearly says, 'No one shall erect a domicile, place of business, factory or other such structure under a City of Winnipeg Bridge.' You'll have to go."

And the mayor turned on his heels and went back to City Council.

The city council agreed that the province had overstepped its authority by appointing an official troll, and they authorized the mayor to remove the troll's fine new house.

The next day the mayor watched with satisfaction as a bulldozer knocked over the fine new Habitation for Humanity house and loaded it onto a City of Winnipeg garbage truck and hauled it away.

"You won't get away with this," the young woman and all her children said to the mayor. "Now we'll shiver in the fall and freeze in the winter and die in the flooding in the spring.

And then the province will simply appoint another official troll."

"We'll see about that," the mayor said and he watched as the police dragged the young woman and her children away to a police car and drove off with the sirens wailing.

Then all the city employees went on strike and there was no garbage removal. There were more mosquitoes than ever before in history. A national poll selected the mayor as the meanest mayor in all of Canada, and the driving home show on radio had so many phone calls about the mayor that the switchboard couldn't handle them all. The mayor lost to Brian Mulroney in a popularity poll.

The week before the election, the mayor sat in his fine leather chair in his big, warm office and considered the fact that he would certainly lose the election. He had fallen behind the Marxist-Leninists and the Rhinoceros party in the polls. His own cat wouldn't let him stroke it. He got into his Lincoln Town Car and drove west on Portage Avenue

"Well," the mayor said to himself, "if I am going to lose the election, then I can do anything I want this last week." There was a sharp chill in the air as he turned onto the Charleswood Bridge.

When he walked down to the river below the bridge, he found the old woman shivering in the cold fall air. He helped her up the slope and into his car.

"I am going to appoint you as head of the Civic Improvement League," he told her as they drove over to the Redwood Bridge. "And you can live in an apartment on Osborne Street and order in pizza every day."

"Oh, thank you, kind sir. How can I ever repay you?"

"You can vote for me in the election," he said.

"Oh, I certainly will."

A little later he walked down to the river below the Redwood Bridge and saw the beautiful young woman he had met there before, shivering in the cold fall air. He helped her up the slope and into his car.

"I am going to appoint you as head of the Winnipeg Arts

Council," he told her as they drove over to the Midtown Bridge. "And you can live in an apartment on Wolseley Street and eat granola and flax bread."

"Oh, thank you, kind sir. How can I ever repay you?"

"You can vote for me in the election," he said.

"Oh, I certainly will."

When he walked down to the river below the Midtown Bridge, he saw the young woman and her children shivering in the cold fall air. He helped them up the slope and into his car.

"I am going to appoint you as head of the Children's Welfare Fund," he told her as they drove to his office at City Hall. "And you can live in a house on Kilkenny Drive and barbecue steaks in your back yard."

"Oh, thank you, kind sir. How can I ever repay you?"

"You can vote for me in the election," he said.

"Oh, I certainly will."

Then the city employees went back to work, and the garbage collectors collected all the garbage, and the mosquitoes stopped biting. The mayor was re-elected in the election. The province agreed that it had overstepped its jurisdiction, and from that day to this, all the trolls under all the bridges in Winnipeg are directly appointed by the mayor himself.

The Villain of the Piece

GLENN WILSON HAD NEVER EXPECTED TO FIND HIMSELF THE villain of the piece and he wasn't sure that he quite deserved the role. It had started as a joke. One night his daughter Karen had read him a notice from the paper. It said "Make yourself famous. Be a character in fiction." And it gave a number to call.

"It's a fundraiser," he said. "Sure as hell. They'll want five hundred bucks and somebody will dedicate a short story to me."

"Phone," Karen said. "Just give it a try. It'll be fun."

And so he phoned. It wasn't quite a fundraiser, the woman who answered told him. Her voice was low and husky with something musical in it. She sounded like what he imagined Daisy in *The Great Gatsby* would have sounded like. It was too complicated to explain on the phone, she said. She'd have to explain it in person. Could he meet for coffee on Thursday? At Oscar's?

He could. He would. He did. "It's more than a fundraiser," he'd told Karen. "It has to be some sort of more elaborate scam."

Now he waited in the coffee room, watching the crowd for the woman. She'd be pretty, he decided. The scam wouldn't work unless she was pretty. Whatever scam it was. Glenn was manager of a chain of grocery stores, and thought of himself as level-headed. Whenever he had a chance to talk about how successful he was, he credited that success to common sense, though sometimes when he was alone he thought it was probably more luck than anything else.

Glenn was completely unprepared for what happened next. The woman materialized at his table as if there had been an excess of ectoplasm at just that spot and she had used it to take form. She was unbelievably slender, so thin she might have been anorexic except that her body also seemed muscular. She wore a loose-fitting white sundress. Her hair was blonde, and she looked as if she had just come out of the shower, except that the hair hung in delicate curls. It must have taken a hairdresser hours to attain that effect. If this was a scam, it was going to be an expensive scam.

"Glenn Wilson?" she asked, though *asked* is probably the wrong word. She said his name as if it were a name of tremendous importance, a name that had never been given its due until she spoke it.

"Yes."

"Come," she said. "Please. There's someone here I want to avoid." And her fingers just touched his hand, as if she had planned to pull him from his chair and had decided against it at the last moment.

He followed her through the crowd of coffee drinkers to the door. They all looked like junior business people, taking their proper coffee breaks, except for a heavy-set man with white hair and a white beard who was scribbling in a notebook in the corner near the window. Glenn paused, and the man gave him a look of sheer, concentrated hatred.

"Daisy," she said, after they were seated in the little Turkish greasy spoon just down the street and around the corner. "Daisy Jordan. And no jokes. I've had enough jokes to last a lifetime about it. My name was Daisy Sigurdson and I married a man named Ralph Jordan. *Voilà*, Daisy Jordan."

"You look like her," Glenn said. "Even your voice sounds like hers."

"No," she answered. "First, this is the only voice I've got, so I have to use it. And all the novel says is that her voice was thrilling. What's that supposed to mean? And if you read the book carefully, you'll notice that she's a flapper. She's got short, dark, straight hair. Fitzgerald didn't even create her. He got her out of a magazine ad for the 1922 Dodge. She's sitting on the fender, smoking a cigarette."

"I'm sorry," Glenn said, though he wasn't sure what he was sorry about. He wished she wasn't so pretty, or that her voice wasn't quite so husky. He wished she wasn't involved in some sort of scam.

"You were right," she said when the waiter brought them coffee. "It is a fundraiser." The waiter was a hefty dark-haired man with thick eyebrows. He stood by the table until she told him, "That's fine, Andris. Everything is okay."

"He's a Latvian," Daisy explained after he had gone. "Or an Estonian or something. One of those Baltic races. He wants to be friendly, but he doesn't know how. He just stands looking at you until you tell him to go." Over in the corner, a woman dressed as a gypsy was laying out a deck of Tarot cards.

"Tell me about the fundraiser," Glenn said. "Nelways makes donations to a variety of charities. I'll ask our public relations officer to take a special look at your request."

"Not Nelways," she said. "You. A thousand bucks, and you get to be the hero of a short story. Of course, it's only your name. It's not really you. And the story gets published, and you can read it to your friends."

"Where does it get published?"

"In a magazine. The money goes to help pay the printing bill."

"And you write the story?"

"Oh God, no. Do I look like a writer? No, you get a real bona fide writer with several books to his credit."

"The big guy with the beard?" he asked. "The guy you didn't want to see at Oscar's?"

"Yes," she said. "Him. David."

"Why didn't he talk to me himself? Why did he ask you to do it?"

"Because he said you wouldn't give him a thousand dollars," she said. "I'm on the board of the magazine. He asked me to do it. So how about it?"

"I'll have to think," Glenn said. "He didn't look very friendly to me. Is he a particular friend of yours?"

"He's a sort of friend," Daisy said. Glenn noticed that she had the most perfect complexion he had ever seen. She seemed almost edible.

"Anyway, I've done my part. I asked you. Now you have to say either yes or no." She glanced at her watch. "And I'm going riding with Margie in a half hour, so I've got to leave." She opened her purse and began to rummage around in it as if it contained something that would confirm her need to leave. She took out a card and scribbled a number on the back. "I'm going out to Gimli to the cottage. Phone me there and let me know."

She passed him the card, and he glanced at the name on it. It said "Stephen Jordan, Consultant," and it gave an address on Park Boulevard. When Glenn glanced up to say goodbye, Daisy was gone, as if she'd run out of ectoplasm and had had to dissolve into the air.

Back at the office, Glenn couldn't concentrate. Somebody wanted to talk to him about vegetables, and all he could think about was blonde hair that looked as if it were wet and a perfect white complexion. He could remember all the parts of Daisy, but he couldn't remember what she looked like with all the parts together.

At home that night, Glenn thought about how perfect his life was. His wife was still beautiful at fifty, and he loved her very much. His house was the perfect house and his job was the perfect job. His Jeep was exactly the car he wanted, and even the bougainvillea he had bought at Shelmerdine's had finally started to bloom. But blonde hair and a perfect complexion, with just a hint of pink in the cheeks, he was sure he remembered a flush, but it might have been just at the moment she spoke about the writer.

"So, Dad," Karen said. "What's the deal?"

"It is a fundraiser," he told her. "You give them a donation, and they put your name in a story."

"Great," she said. "Go for it."

"How much do they want?" his wife asked.

"Two hundred and fifty dollars," Glenn lied. And he wondered whether he'd have to tell more lies.

"That's a lot of money for some plain foolishness," his wife said. "What if he makes you the villain of the piece?"

"Fine," Glenn said. "Then I'll be a villain."

He didn't call for a whole week, but by then his food had lost all its taste and his eyes wouldn't stay on a balance sheet. He seemed to have forgotten how to read numbers. He phoned the number in Gimli.

"Great," Daisy said when he announced he was going to donate a thousand dollars. "That's terrific."

"I just happen to be driving up to Gimli today," he told her. "I could drop the cheque off at your place."

"No," she said, "not today. I've got some people up today. Tomorrow at two."

Glenn thought he ought to tell her he wasn't going to be in Gimli tomorrow, that it was only a coincidence he was going to be there today and that he was not driving up specifically to see her, but instead he only answered, "Two o'clock will be fine."

The directions Daisy had given Glenn turned out to be more than a little confused. He found himself hopelessly lost on a road that led through marshes. Ahead, it looked barely passable, even for a Jeep. He stopped and got out, but at that very moment a Honda Accord splashed its way through the mud in front of him and pulled up beside him. There were two hopelessly beautiful people in the car. Glenn was certain he had seen the man on television, and he knew he'd seen the woman in the fashion section of the newspaper.

"Daisy is only five minutes away," the man said, "but don't stop even for a second, or you're finished." Glenn didn't know whether the man was talking about the road or about Daisy.

"She's the craziest woman in the world," the man went on, "but we love her. Take care." And they bounced on down the mud road.

Daisy was wearing white sailor's pants and a white halter with a huge straw hat that made her look tiny. She was on the deck of the largest cottage Glenn had ever seen. Beyond it, the lake gleamed blue and silver. She invited him in and offered him a martini. She already had a glass of her own. The remains of lunch were strewn on the table: bagels and salmon and fruit and a couple of empty martini glasses.

Glenn took the martini, and handed her the cheque. She put it in a drawer without even looking at it. The deck ran all the way around the cottage, and the interior of the building seemed cool and cavernous. The sun beat down on Glenn's neck, but Daisy seemed perfectly cool.

"It's hot," Daisy said, and Glenn thought, "*Hot. Hot. Hot.*"

"Yes," he said, "it's hot."

"We should go look at the pelicans," Daisy said, as if that were the reason Glenn had come. She led him to a small canal he hadn't noticed when he arrived. There was a powerful boat with a huge black motor on it parked there. Daisy roared the motor into life and the wash piled waves up both sides of the canal.

"Crow Island," she shouted over the roar of the motor as the boat leaped into the open lake. Ahead, a narrow spit of land, hardly more than a sandbar, lay low on the water. A line of white on the bar resolved itself into hundreds of pelicans and gulls. They took off as the boat approached, and the air was so full of white flying things that it looked like a travelogue about Africa. Daisy circled the island, then suddenly aimed the boat directly at a beach on the far side. She approached so fast that it looked as if she intended to try to go right over the land, but she cut the motor at the last instant, and the boat rode the wash into a delicate landing right on the shore.

Daisy took Glenn's hand and they walked along the shore towards a clump of willows and a couple of taller trees. All along the shore, sandpipers and yellowlegs ran in front of them, or took off whimpering over the blue lake. Wild raspberries grew in profusion higher up, and the beach was covered with large white shells with purple linings.

When they reached a small indentation, a bay within a bay where the water was clean and deep and clear, Daisy sat down on the sand and took off her sandals. Glenn, who was still dressed for work in a jacket and tie, felt ridiculous. He took off his jacket and his Oxfords and his socks.

"I'm going for a swim," Daisy said, and there, directly in front of him, she took off all her clothes and dived into the water. In the second before the dive, her hair curled around her shoulders so that she looked exactly like Venus in the Botticelli painting. Glenn hesitated only a moment, then he took off his clothes and joined her in the clear blue water. Afterwards, they made love on the sand, and Glenn felt that if his life were to end, that would be the perfect moment.

But it didn't end, of course. Nothing ever works out that easy. He agreed to meet her again in exactly one week, and he went home and lied to his wife and he lied to his daughter and he lied to the people at work. He cursed his former reliability, because it made it almost impossible to conduct an affair without people noticing.

Daisy phoned him at work on Tuesday. Her husband, the consultant, had gone off to Japan to consult. She was bored. Could he come out today?

It was really impossible. Glenn had appointments all day long. He'd already rescheduled too many things so that he could be free on Thursday.

Daisy said she was sorry and hung up. Glenn tried to concentrate on special coupon offers and the dispute between the butchers at the Grant Park store, but he kept imagining clear water and blonde hair, and by noon it was obvious he was not going to get anything done anyway. He dialled her number in Gimli and waited while the phone rang eight times. Finally, a male voice answered.

"Hello, can I help you?"

"May I speak to Daisy?" Glenn asked.

"How did you get this number?" the voice asked. "This is an unlisted number."

"Daisy gave it to me," Glenn said. "Now may I please speak to her?"

There was a moment of silence, the kind of muted silence that means someone has covered the receiver with his hand and is speaking to someone else. Finally, the voice said, "I'm sorry. Daisy is unable to come to the phone. Good-bye." And the line went dead with a click.

It had started to rain by the time Glenn got to his car, but that did not deter him. He drove recklessly, far too fast through Clandeboye and Petersfield and Winnipeg Beach, ignoring the signs that told him the speed limit was fifty kilometres. He almost went off the mud road into the marshes on the last stretch.

When he got to the cottage, nobody answered his knock on the door. He walked around the deck to the side that faced the lake, and there was Daisy sitting in the rain in an Adirondack chair, crying. She slipped into his arms, wetting his shirt, and Glenn was infuriated with himself that he was fastidious enough to notice.

The problem, she said, was David. He'd told her that she was going to have to get rid of Glenn.

"He said you've already got your thousand bucks' worth even if he doesn't write the story. He's going to make you look bad. Not evil or anything, just dumb. He's going to call the story 'The Villain of the Piece' or something like that." Her voice was even huskier than usual, as if she had the beginnings of a cold.

"He can write whatever he wants," Glenn reassured Daisy.

"But he can't keep me away from you. Besides, isn't that the husband's job, driving away suitors?"

"I don't think my husband would notice if I kept a harem of men in the spare bedroom," Daisy said. "And I guess I've sort of had a thing going with David for the last few years. And he doesn't want you around."

"That was him on the phone?" Glenn asked. "The guy with the white beard and hair that I saw at Oscar's?"

"Yes."

"He's twice your age and overweight in the bargain. How did you ever link up with him?"

"It was a Junior League fundraiser. For cancer. He came and read a couple of stories, and he ended up at the same table as me. I guess that's how I find men, through fundraisers." Her hair was stringy from the rain, and Glenn noticed for the first time that her eyes were not blue but green.

"But why him? Surely you could have had any man you wanted?"

"He asked. I was bored, and he asked me to sleep with him, so I did. He calls me his muse, and that was kind of flattering for a while. He says all the women in his stories are based on me."

"And where is he now?"

"He's gone for a walk. He wants to talk to you when he comes back. He wants to send you away."

"We'll see who sends who away," Glenn told her, but before he could say any more, a large man in a Tilley hat with the edges curled up appeared around the point and started walking down the beach toward him. The man seemed to favour his right knee, and he carried a stick that he used like a cane. He stopped and sat on a large rock, and Glenn walked down to meet him.

As Glenn approached, the man took a manuscript from his pocket, and he handed it to Glenn. Glenn took it wordlessly and began to read.

The story began, "Glenn Wilson had never expected to be the villain of the piece." It went on to detail Glenn's relationship with Daisy, their coffee at the Turkish restaurant, their lovemaking at Crow Island. It left nothing out. It even named his wife and his daughter and his secretary at work.

"She told you everything?" Glenn asked.

"She's my muse," the man said. "We have no secrets. And of course there's a certain amount of research involved. Details are important."

"And you're going to publish this?" Glenn could imagine the response his friends and the people at work would have.

"Well, that depends on you," the man said. "If you go away and promise never to get in touch with Daisy again, then I'll put you in a story about a man who has a heart transplant. Good muses are hard to find these days, and I don't know whether I've got the energy to go find another one."

"I have to think," Glenn said, and he went to his car and drove back to Winnipeg. When he got home, his wife was still beautiful and his daughter was lively and full of fun. The next day, his secretary, Miss Harding, arranged all his appointments, and the quarterly report said that Nelways had never done better. He couldn't imagine how his life could be improved.

Or at least, he couldn't imagine anything better until Thursday. Then he phoned Daisy, and drove out to Gimli, and they made love beside the pelicans. For the rest of the summer, he drove out three times a week, and left Nelways Supermarkets to their own devices. He was tanned from spending so much time in the sun, but he told his wife and daughter that he was taking long walks at noon for his health, and they believed him.

Then one day in September he came into his office, and the atmosphere was different. People were looking at him in an odd way, and there seemed an almost mysterious giddiness in the place. Workers gathered in twos and threes and read to each other from a magazine. Glenn went to McNally Robinson's bookstore at lunch and bought a copy. The text was nearly the same as the manuscript he had read, but it brought the affair with Daisy up to date, and it was graphic in its descriptions. He hadn't known that magazines were allowed to publish that much detail.

Glenn decided not to go back to the office that afternoon. He couldn't take the barely disguised jokes at his expense. Instead, he went home to find a moving truck just taking away the last of the furniture. His wife was gone, but she had left a long note explaining how mean his betrayal of her had been, and expressing the hope that she would never see him again. His daughter phoned to tell him that he was beyond contempt.

Glenn drove the now familiar road to Gimli, but he drove more slowly than he had ever done before. Daisy had told him that her husband would be home for one of his infrequent visits. Glenn didn't know what he would say if her husband answered the door. Probably he'd have to tell him that he was in love with Daisy and had come to take her away.

When Glenn got to the road that led through the marshes to Daisy's cottage, the road was gone. A dragline and a bulldozer were parked near the highway, but where the road had been was only a broad stretch of swamp. Glenn thought for a moment that he must have taken a wrong turn, but he knew it was something more than that. The sun was just setting, and it would soon be dusk.

He drove into the town and parked his car by the hotel. Then he walked out to the end of the pier that stretched into Lake Winnipeg. At the end of the pier, a figure sat hunched, looking over the water towards a green light at the south point of the bay.

"The road is gone," Glenn told the figure.

"Yes," the man replied. "Her husband came home. Someone showed him the story, and he's taken her away."

"Where has he taken her?" Glenn asked.

"I don't know," the other replied. "Someplace where rich people gather. In no time she'll be in love with someone else. And we'll go on, you and I, living our own dull little lives."

"Is there more to the story?" Glenn asked.

"No," the heavy-set man said. "This is it. Once the muse is gone, the story is over."

Then the darkness, which had been gathering in Europe, leaped the Atlantic, flooded Newfoundland and Quebec, broke across Ontario and submerged them in darkness. The green light flickered and went out.

Pandora

IT'S EASY ENOUGH TO SAY NOW THAT THEY SHOULD HAVE
noticed that something was bothering the cat, but both Jackie
and Patty had more on their minds on that particular
Thursday than a twenty-one-year-old cat named Pandora.
Jackie had just been fired that very morning from her job with
the Manitoba Theatre Exchange after fifteen years as head
costume designer.

"What am I going to do?" she asked Patty. "How many
jobs are there in Winnipeg for costume designers? That's it!
I'm finished. Done for. Kaput."

"Design is design," Patty told her with less sympathy than
she intended or Jackie wanted. "Design something else.
Sweaters for the garment trade. Electric kettles. Railway
trains." She'd just come back from the doctor, who had told
her that she was suffering from CFS, chronic fatigue syndrome,
a disease that she did not believe in and whose sufferers she

despised. Pale youths with pince-nez glasses. Girls with stringy hair and bad teeth.

Pandora, meanwhile, was pondering the box she'd overturned in the sitting room. It had been entirely too enticing for her to ignore, and she blamed both women for leaving it there. Jackie and Patty had bought it at a garage sale from a Greek family in Transcona. It was the kind of wooden box in which braids of garlic are sold, and it said in red lettering, "Pandora's Box." They had made a big ceremony of giving it to her for her birthday, with a lime-green catnip mouse Scotch-taped to it. Then they had just left it in the sitting room.

Of course, Pandora had examined it. Being a cat has its advantages: moments in the sun, the incredible warmth of a mouthful of feathers, the slow blinking moments when the world stops while you make up your mind. But it also has its responsibilities. You have to guarantee that bags are truly empty by walking into them. And you have to know what is inside every box in the house.

Catness Oblige.

"I can't design toasters," Jackie said. "I hate toasters. I hate toast. I don't even like bread."

"At least you can walk," Patty answered. "At least you don't have some grotesque hippy disease."

"What do you mean?"

"I've got CFS. Chronic fatigue syndrome."

"That's yuppie disease."

"Hippie, yuppie, I don't care. The doctor says I have to take things easy. I mustn't exert myself."

"That's crazy. You jog fifty miles a day. You do a million push-ups. You've got a black belt in something. How can you have CFS?"

"Well, I have. I've got a certificate. I have to lie down a lot."

Pandora was worried. When she opened the box, four little furry things scuttled out and hid in the corner of the room under the sideboard. She recognized them at once: Flood, Famine, Pestilence and War. She'd caught Flood, Famine and

War and put them back in the box, but Pestilence had sneaked under the chesterfield, and there was no getting it out. Jackie had sat on the chesterfield and watched the David Letterman show, and the next day she lost her job. Patty had fallen asleep watching Jay Leno, and then she'd come down with CFS.

A couple of years ago it would have been no problem. Pandora would have found the only way out from the chesterfield and she'd have waited, not moving a muscle until she caught the furry creature. But now, after about five minutes, she would fall asleep with her mouth open and even silly field mice sneaked by and ate the crumbs of cheese that Jackie and Patty dropped on the floor.

"Let's go back to Paris," Jackie said. "Let's rent a place on the rue de l'Aude by the Alésia Station and drink wine at little cafés and watch the Canadian tourists buying cheese."

"You're poor," Patty told her. "You're a failed designer with no future and I'm hopelessly crippled by CFS. We can buy a cottage in Winnipeg Beach and sit in cedar Adirondack chairs watching the sun set over Lake Winnipeg, then we'll go to our well-deserved rewards."

"In Winnipeg Beach, the sun does not set over the lake. It rises. We'll have to get up at the crack of dawn."

"Well, so much for that."

Pandora was very tired, but she knew she had to concentrate. She checked out the box, and she could hear the furry creatures scrambling around inside it. Then she went back to the chesterfield and sat very still in front of the small hole the furry thing had made in the lining at the back. She had vowed that she would not fall asleep, but after a few minutes she was back in her kittenhood, stalking a yellow warbler at the base of a willow tree. She was about to pounce when something startled her awake. There, just inches in front of her, was a small greyish thing. Pestilence. Pandora knew it at once. She pounced.

The phone rang. It was the Manitoba Theatre Exchange. They offered Jackie her job back. It had all been a terrible mistake.

"Wonderful," Patty said, and she realized that she felt terrific. She thought she might jog a few miles. Then she'd go to the refit centre and work out on the Nautilus machine for an hour or two.

"I don't have to design toasters," Jackie said. "I don't have to design railway trains."

"That's too bad," Patty said. "The world could do with a decent toaster, not to mention the railway trains."

Pandora had the grey furry thing in her mouth. It didn't taste very good, but then she had no intention of eating it. If she'd been younger, she might have played with it for a while, but she was taking no chances of letting it get away.

Putting it back in the box was another thing entirely. Pandora put her paw on the top of the box and heard the other grey furry things scurrying around. Finally, there was nothing left to do. She opened the box and dropped Pestilence back inside. But before she could close the box, another grey furry thing shot out of the box and headed for the chesterfield. Flood. Pandora slammed the box closed, and in an effort that used up two of her remaining three lives, she caught the furry grey thing by the nape of its neck just as it was about to get into the chesterfield.

But how to get it back into the box? If she opened the box to replace Flood, she might release Famine, or even War.

The large creatures, she thought to herself. The creatures that called themselves Jackie and Patty. They weren't good for much more than opening cans of cat food and cleaning the litter box, which they didn't do nearly often enough, but they were good at opening and closing boxes. She had tried to speak to them years ago, but they were remarkably unintelligent. She had asked politely for a little milk, and they had put her out and left her outside all night. They had run out of catnip, and it had taken weeks to get them to understand the problem. Still, they seemed the only possible solution.

Pandora carried Flood to the kitchen where Jackie and Patty were drinking a cup of tea. They seemed happy, and that was a good sign.

"Could you give me a hand with this creature?" Pandora asked. "It's actually really dangerous, and I think we should put it back in the box."

"She's making that funny chirping sound," Patty said. "I wonder what she wants."

"Oh God," Jackie answered. "She's caught a mouse or a bird. Something disgusting. And she wants to give it to us as a present. I thought she was getting too old for that."

Pandora looked up hopefully.

"It's a mouse," Jackie said. "Or no, not a mouse. A vole, or something like that. We've got to get it out of the house before it gets into the furniture."

"It's Flood," Pandora said. "We must take extreme care."

"Well, she's not going to give it up," Patty said. "I'll take her outside." And she picked up Pandora and carried her out to the end of the garden.

"Let go," she said, squeezing Pandora's jaws.

"No," Pandora would have answered, but under the pressure of Patty's fingers, her mouth opened and the small furry thing scrambled in the grass and hid under the rain barrel by the shed.

The water started to rise in Grand Forks, North Dakota. Pandora watched a film showing it breach the dike on television news that very night. She meowed at the door, hoping that Patty or Jackie would let her out so she could get the thing from under the rain barrel.

"You're too old to be spending the night outside," Jackie told her. "Here, I'll give you a little catnip, and you can go out tomorrow if it's sunny."

Pandora had been trying to give up catnip. It always gave her a headache the next day, and she lost track of time.

The next day it rained, and it rained the day after, too. The flood surrounded Emerson, and Pandora looked out the gloomy window. On the weekend, Ste. Agathe was flooded. Pandora could see from her window that the furry thing had got into the rain barrel and was swimming around. Town after town was evacuated, but Jackie and Patty wouldn't let Pandora outside.

"We've just got a twenty-four-hour alert," Patty told Pandora when she meowed at the door one morning. "If we have to move out, I don't want to spend the final hours looking for an old, lost cat. Go catch a mouse or something."

The television said they were building a dike forty kilometres long, but it might not be enough to save Winnipeg. The water would back up into the La Salle River, and then everyone would be flooded. The small furry thing was now swimming frantically in the rain barrel. Pandora could see just the spot where she would be able to sit and scoop it out as it swam by.

And then the house was full of people. First they carried everything from the basement up to the main floor. Then they carried up as many things as they could from the main floor to the second floor. Someone put Pandora in a cage and set her out on the back steps. She could see that the river had come over its banks and was right up into the garden.

"Adrian and Mitch, you go play in the back yard," someone with a big man's voice said. "Everybody is tripping over you."

"Okay," Adrian said. "Come on, Mitch." Adrian was ten, and Mitch was nine, but they looked so much alike that sometimes people thought they were twins. Mitch was carrying the box with the lettering that said Pandora's Box.

"Be careful with that," Pandora told him. "There's dangerous stuff in there."

"I'll be careful," Mitch said. "I'm always careful."

"I wonder if you'd mind letting me out for a moment?" Pandora asked. "It's terribly uncomfortable in this cage."

"Okay," Mitch said. "But you have to promise not to run away. I'll get in deep trouble if you do."

"I promise," Pandora told him.

"Who are you talking to?" Adrian asked from the edge of the river.

"The cat."

"Cats can't talk," Adrian said. "Everybody knows that."

"This one can," Mitch said, opening the cage and letting

Pandora out. In a second, Pandora was at the top of the rain barrel. She scooped up the furry thing as it swam past and carried it back towards the cage.

"You let the cat out," Adrian said. "We better get someone to catch her, or we'll be grounded for a week." And he ran into the house.

"Quick," Pandora told Mitch. "Put this one in the box, but don't let the others out."

Mitch picked up the grey furry thing by its tail, and dropped it into the box.

"Now, put the box into the river before it's too late."

"Why . . . ?" Mitch began, but Pandora hushed him.

"I'll explain later," Pandora said. "Just do what I ask."

Mitch was a little unsure, but he launched the box into the river at the bottom of the garden. The current swirled it away, and in a moment it was gone.

"Okay, what was that all about?" Mitch asked, but Pandora just winked at him and said meow.

Patty and Jackie ran out into the garden where Mitch and Pandora were sitting, watching the river. Adrian followed them.

"I think it's starting to go down," Adrian said.

"You're right," Jackie said. "You can see the wet mark on the tree where it used to be." There was no doubt about it. The river was receding even as they watched.

Patty picked up Pandora and began to stroke her. "Paris sounds like a good idea," she said to Jackie. "If we could only find somebody to take care of Pandora while we're gone."

"Me," said Mitch. "I'll take care of her."

"Me, too," said Adrian. "We'll both take care of her."

And by the time Jackie and Patty had bought their tickets, the box with the furry things had bobbed past Lockport and Selkirk and out into Lake Winnipeg. When they landed in Paris it was sailing down the Nelson River towards Hudson Bay. It came out into the North Atlantic just as they were drinking wine at a small café in the Fourteenth Arrondissement. They flew right over it on their way back to Canada.

Pandora sat between Adrian and Mitch in their back yard, under a hot prairie sun. A yellow warbler landed a few feet from her nose, but she didn't even blink. Somewhere in the world, Flood, Famine, Pestilence and War went about their work, but where the three of them sat, there was only the smell of lilacs.

Trader Joe's

THE MAN LYING ON THE SIDEWALK AT THE ENTRANCE TO
Trader Joe's looked like a nice man. He was wearing a light,
short-sleeved white shirt and red pants. He still had most of
his hair, though it was thin and white, and you could see his
scalp. His skin was blotched with brown liver spots, and he
was bleeding from his forehead where it had hit the sidewalk.
The pavement was splattered with drops of blood. The drops
were very red, so red that they muted all the other colours of
the people walking by, the cars in the parking lot, the distant
brown mountains.

He wasn't moving, but he was talking in a soft voice to the
clerk from Trader Joe's who was comforting him with low,
cooed murmurs. Greg could hear the wail of a siren in the distance, but it was far too soon to be coming for the man on the
sidewalk. He had just fallen, and there had been no time to
call an ambulance. Greg guessed that the man was in his

nineties. He looked like a proud man, but he couldn't feel proud, lying there on the sidewalk.

The man looked anxious, though not in pain. He was probably worried about how much trouble he was going to be. Somebody would have to come and get him, and they would have to get the car back to the condominium. Then he'd have to lie in bed for a couple of days. His wife wouldn't want him to go shopping by himself any more, and they probably wouldn't let him drive again, either.

Greg didn't stop, because the Trader Joe's clerk seemed to have things under control. There was nothing he could do. To stay and watch would be morbid curiosity, and Greg was Canadian enough not to want to invade the man's private grief.

The car parked beside Greg was a Jaguar, and next to it was a Mercedes Benz. Directly in front of him was a SAAB convertible. Had the man been driving one of these cars? Greg glanced back at the entrance to Trader Joe's. The man was still lying on the sidewalk. People walked in and out of the store, paying no attention to him. Greg's sweater was in the back seat, and he wondered whether he shouldn't fold it up and take it over to the man and put it under his head, which was still lying on the hard cement. But he didn't. It would create too many problems. He didn't care about the sweater, but other people would, and he would be involved in a way that he didn't want to be.

Sheila was waiting for him at the dress shop on El Paseo where he had dropped her off. Or she would be waiting for him in fifteen minutes. He drove slowly around the parking lot, then, on an impulse, he stopped and went into Pier One Imports. He could see the entrance to Trader Joe's from there, but he couldn't tell whether the man was still lying on the sidewalk. There was nothing in Pier One that he wanted. Once, he had been attracted to carved elephants from Indonesia and wicker furniture, and iron candle holders, but he no longer cared about them.

Maybe the man was dying. Maybe he had had a heart

attack, or was having one when Greg walked by him. The man had looked like someone who had been important in his day, and he might know he was dying and worry about all the things he hadn't got around to doing.

It was hot when Greg left the store and got into his little rented Chevrolet Caprice. He could hear another siren in the distance, and he was aware then that he could almost always hear sirens in the distance. He knew that when he got home to Winnipeg, he would remember Palm Desert as a place where you could always hear sirens, low-pitched rumours of disaster at the edges of consciousness.

Sheila led him to a place called Tommy Bahama's on the second floor of a shopping mall. It was a new shopping mall, but almost all the stores were empty. She had met a man walking around the mall and he had recommended it to her. He and his wife were going there for the second time. Sheila had bought a new blouse, and she opened the bag to show it to Greg. Greg said he thought it was nice, though he really couldn't see it in the darkness of the bag.

Greg told Sheila about the man on the sidewalk, but he told the story badly, and he could tell that it didn't interest her. Everybody here is dying, she told him. They have come here to die. The only people who are not dying are the Mexicans, who do the work.

We're all dying, Greg told her, but it was a cliché, and it didn't have any effect. He wondered how he would feel if he were lying on a sidewalk seeing his own blood and watching the people hurry by him.

"Have you noticed the number of gay men there are in this part of town?" Sheila asked, and Greg was startled. He hadn't thought about it, but suddenly he noticed that almost all the men in the restaurant who were under seventy seemed to be dressed and made up as if they were playing gay men in a movie. Greg did not want to notice this, and he felt again that he was invading their privacy by thinking that they were gay.

They ordered crab cakes and a spinach salad, which they shared. Greg was facing the wall, though he could see people come and go as they came from the inside section to the out-side section where you ate under umbrellas. Sheila could see all the people, and she told Greg about them. He had to twist around in his chair to see them, and they stared back at him as if they thought he were rude. Sheila pointed out a couple directly behind Greg. He had seen the woman while they were ordering. She had walked by several times, looking for some-one. She was tall and large-boned, about sixty-five years old, he had guessed, and she carried herself as if she were used to authority. Still, there was a kind of carefulness in her walk that made him think she had been drinking. Now, she was sitting with a young Mexican man with a round hat and a smooth, beautiful face. He was talking to her in a low, intense voice, though Greg could not make out any of the words. The woman glared at Greg, but the man paid no attention and went on in his intense monologue.

Greg wondered if the man was still on the sidewalk, or if by now he were comfortable in a soft bed with people bring-ing him cool things to drink. Another woman entered and joined the pair behind him. At first, Greg thought she was very young, because her hair was blonde and her body was the body of a young woman. But as she passed, he could see that her face was set in a mask that struck him as very old. It didn't look like a face that could have expressions, but when he turned around a few minutes later, she was laughing, and she looked young again.

Sheila wanted to do some more shopping and told Greg to take the car and go back to the condominium. She could walk. It was only a couple of miles, and the weather was beau-tiful. Greg said that he wanted to look at a couple of the shops, a kitchen store and a place that specialized in Navajo jewellery and silver. If she wanted a ride, she could meet him at the fountain in an hour.

The kitchen store was filled with beautiful things, but everything was way too expensive, and if it wasn't too expen-sive it was too heavy to take back on the plane. All around him, the people were in wonderful physical shape. The men seemed athletic and flat-bellied. The women were graceful and elegant, and they were dressed in bright outdoor clothes. But all the faces had the same strange aspect. It was as if the students of a progressive university had suddenly been hit by some disease that aged their faces terribly, while leaving their bodies intact, or as if they had struck some flawed deal with the devil that had given them a limited form of immortality.

"They come here to die," Sheila told him that evening as he barbecued steaks. The lawn behind the condominium blended with the thirteenth hole of a golf course, but it was dark now, and the golfers had quit for the day. "This is like an elephant's graveyard. All these people are staving off death with exercise and nutrition and expensive medical care and face lifts and tummy tucks. This is the good life. If you're very lucky and very rich, this is how you get to die. Surrounded by sunlight and hummingbirds and Alfa Romeos."

Sheila had walked home. She had decided that she would meet him, but a clerk in the store where she had bought a pair of shorts had spent a long time on the telephone, and so she was a few minutes late and the hour had passed. Greg had already gone, and at first she was unjustifiably angry with him, though it wasn't his fault. "I'm always late," she told him. "You have to allow me five minutes."

The man from the condominium next door was smoking a cigar, and the scent drifted over to them, strangely sweet and acrid at the same time. He sat from morning to night on the same chair, dressed in only a pair of shorts. His body was tanned so dark that he was almost black. He was an auto dealer from Regina, he had told them the first day. He was recovering from a heart attack, and had to take it easy. The cigar was his way of quitting smoking. He got up now and walked over to them. "Sorry about the smoke," he said. "I don't like to smoke inside and sometimes it drifts over and annoys other people. Just tell me if it bothers you, and I'll quit."

Both Greg and Sheila said no, it was fine, though they had each complained to the other about the smell. "I've got a touch of indigestion," the man said. "I think I'll call it a day. See you tomorrow."

But he didn't. The next day he was dead. They had heard sirens in the night, but they always heard sirens, and they had not thought much about it. He had left them and gone into his house and died. His wife had discovered him dead on the floor when she came home from her bridge club at about eleven o'clock. His chair was still in its place with his ashtray on the grass beside it when they looked out the sliding glass doors the next morning.

"He was old," Sheila said. "He was sick. He had been waiting for death, and now it has happened."

"What are we doing here?" Greg asked her. "Is this a trial run for us? Are we the same as those people?"

"Don't be ridiculous," Sheila answered. "We're here for a holiday. We've got three weeks, then it's back to the grind. We aren't ever going to be able to retire and live here."

The United States had been bombing Iraq for several weeks now, sporadic attacks on radar installations, and there were reports nearly every day in the newspapers, dutiful notations about just what had been bombed. Greg wondered how Iraq could continue to maintain so many places that needed bombing. Then, the day after the man next door died, the president announced that they would begin bombing the Serbs. Greg tried to calculate the expense of all the bombing, but it was a hopeless task. He couldn't decide whether he approved of the bombing or not.

Sheila had taken to hiking in the mountains for exercise. Every morning, she would drive to the Indian Canyons and hike along the trails. The neighbours warned her against cougars and rattlesnakes, but she laughed and said that all she ever saw were ground squirrels and quail and the odd hiker doing the same thing that she was. Greg did not fear the wild animals, but he did worry that one of those hikers would turn out to be a serial murderer, and he might never see his wife again. He didn't tell her this, but she knew what he thought anyway, and she told him not to worry.

The small courtyard behind the condominium had a lemon tree that was in flower, though it still had a lot of lemons on it. Greg didn't know whether he was allowed to pick the lemons or not, but he picked them anyway and used them in his drinks. The bougainvillea that clambered up the arbour between their condominium and the next was startlingly red, and it attracted large hummingbirds with purple heads and smaller, iridescent green hummingbirds, hardly larger than a moth. The scent of flowers was everywhere, and certain breezes would suddenly fill his nose and he would feel that he had very nearly remembered something important that he had forgotten.

Sheila came down from the mountain, safe for another day. She had met some people whom she had known a long time ago, before she had met Greg, and she had invited them for dinner. Greg went out and bought a salmon, and he cooked it in aluminum foil with a lot of dill and fresh lemon. Sheila made a salad with a citrus vinaigrette, and she baked a lemon pie for dessert.

The couple who came to dinner seemed a lot older than they, but Greg didn't even try to find out how old they actually were. The man, Chris, had been an historian for the Parks Board, and he had retired early. His wife, Susan, had worked for an advertising agency. She still worked for them on a freelance basis. They were touring historic sites in the American west and writing articles, which were syndicated in a lot of rural newspapers in western Canada. They would be impossible to tell from anybody else in Palm Desert in a restaurant. They had the same air of tragic good health he saw everywhere. He imagined that if Chris fell asleep in a lawn chair in the sun, he would sleep with his mouth open.

The light bulb in the kitchen burned out just as Sheila was preparing supper, and Greg replaced it with the only other bulb he could find, a bulb that must have been designed for outdoors, because it was terribly bright. Under its cruel light, Greg could see the lines around Sheila's eyes, and the powder on her cheeks seemed mottled and patched. She had rubbed her eyes, and her eye shadow was streaked. Even her hair seemed thinner, and he could see the scalp below.

Back in the dim light of the dining room, Sheila looked as pretty as ever. Chris and Susan laughed easily. They had gone birding at the Salton Sea. Greg wondered at the word. He had heard of bird watching, but the term *birding* somehow made it seem professional and important, not something you would do just for fun. They had seen a white-faced ibis and seemed to think that was an important find.

Susan and Chris wanted to talk about Kosovo and the bombing. Chris was worried about the historic sites that would be ruined, and Susan was concerned about the environment, about the animals that were dying needlessly, the dogs and cats abandoned as refugees fled into Macedonia. They turned on the television and saw pictures of Serbians in hospital, but the Serbs had banished all the western reporters, and the pictures they saw were provided by the Serbian government. There were pictures of bombed buildings and fires and rockets in the nighttime sky, but any of the pictures of the damage could have been left over from the bombing in Iraq.

At three o'clock in the morning, Greg woke up with a headache. They had all had too much to drink, and he wandered out to survey the wreckage. Somehow, they had finished the bottle of Scotch, and all four bottles of wine that Greg had bought just hours before dinner. He went to the washroom and took an aspirin, then, on reflection, he took another. Still he couldn't sleep. He had strange wakeful dreams in which he tried to make his way around a building where all the doors led him farther away from where he wanted to go.

By five in the morning, it was clear that he was not going to sleep, so he got up and ate a grapefruit. His body felt stiff and sore, and his old trick knee gave way and he nearly fell walking from the kitchen to the dining area. He watched the light begin to brighten on the golf course, and the palm trees changed from indistinct monsters into tropical greenery. A short while later, the first golfers arrived in their little electric cars. This was the thirteenth hole, Greg thought. They must have driven their first strokes into the blackness of night.

Sheila woke late, and she was out of sorts. She did not usually drink much, and she had certainly not intended to drink as much as she had drunk last night. She blamed Greg for relentlessly filling everybody's glass as soon as it was half-empty. It was embarrassing, she said. We hardly know these people and we all talked far too much about our intimate lives. Greg didn't remember saying anything very intimate, but he didn't want to start a quarrel, so he just said that he was sorry.

The sun was brilliant as usual. The hummingbirds were back again, and this time, Greg found a book about birds and identified the large one with the purple head as an Anna's hummingbird. He was quite proud of himself, and in the next few minutes he identified a mockingbird, a verdin and a Bewick's wren. Sheila went for her walk in the mountains, even though she did not feel like it. Through the years of their marriage, Greg had discovered that she was the kind of woman who punished herself for things she did that she thought were wrong, like getting drunk or sick. He himself did whatever he could to avoid consequences.

Sheila got back and took a shower. She made egg salad sandwiches for lunch, and then she settled down to read her book. Greg was restless. He felt like lying down and taking a nap, but he didn't want to go to sleep. He thought that if he went to sleep he would feel like he was falling, something that had happened to him all his life whenever he tried to take a nap, and so he almost never slept in the day.

"I'm going to replenish the booze supply," Greg shouted to Sheila where she lay reading in the chaise longue by the edge of the golf course.

"Don't bother on my behalf," she answered, and went on reading.

Greg parked quite a long way from Trader Joe's, because the lot was nearly full. The mall was very busy, and people hurried in and out of the store. Greg found a bottle of Scotch and a couple of bottles of wine and stood patiently in a long line to pay for them. The clerk put the bottles in small brown bags inside a larger brown bag, and wished Greg a good day.

Just as Greg was stepping out onto the sidewalk, a woman in a hurry brushed him with a shopping cart. Greg turned to avoid her, and he either stepped on an uneven piece of sidewalk, or his bad knee gave way again, and he felt himself fall heavily to the pavement. This must be what happened to the old man, he thought as he fell. He heard a loud noise, and his head filled with colours.

When he opened his eyes, he could see the bright red drops of blood on the sidewalk. He could hear a mourning dove somewhere in the distance, but the dove's moan turned into a flow of words from the clerk who leaned over him. Greg's red pants were torn where his knee had hit the sidewalk, and he could see the brown liver spots on his arm and the thin, stretched skin over the back of his hand. One of the wine bottles had broken as he fell, and the liquid made a small purple lake in the gutter. He felt that if he wanted, he could fall asleep without trouble.

He thought of Sheila back at the condominium. Someone would have to phone her, and everything was going to be very complicated. He didn't know whether he had enough insurance. He imagined that he was standing a little way from the sidewalk watching, only the man on the ground was not him but the old man he had seen fall the other day.

The smell of orange blossoms was almost smothering. The wall of Trader Joe's had become covered with bougainvilleas, as bright red as the blood on the sidewalk. An Anna's hummingbird, its head an iridescent purple, hovered in the air just a couple of feet away. The people entering and leaving the store hurried as if they were embarrassed by having to watch Greg lying on the sidewalk. The clerk continued to coo, and Greg tried to comfort him.

"It's fine," he told the clerk. "Everything is going to be okay. Don't worry."

Prelude to America

SHE SHOULDN'T HAVE DONE IT. SHE SHOULDN'T HAVE LAIN with him there in the sweet meadow, the sun low in the sky, the music still ringing in her ears. So what if he had played on the violin while everyone danced, so what if he sang like an angel? She was only seventeen and he was the father of five children, so what if her blood had flooded her body like a disease, she should have said no, I can find my own way home, thank you. She should have said I am sorry, sir, what you ask is impossible. The nineteenth century had tipped on its fulcrum and they were sliding towards a new century, but there was still plenty of time. She could have said no.

But she didn't. It's a curse on the whole family. We can't say no. When somebody invites us to pleasure, we forget what we were doing, we forget all our plans, and we're thrashing in the bedclothes or crushing the flowers in the sweet meadows. There was plenty of warning. The gulls were crying out danger, the terns were calling beware, beware. The heat of the blood is no excuse, but we make it our excuse again and again.

And that's what Thorunn did in the Icelandic dawn when the century was gathering itself for disaster. She forgot that she could recite whole sections of the Bible, that her father was the priest at Tjorn, that her mother had warned against such a moment. So this is love, she thought, and she slipped out of her dress as if it had no buttons, as if it had been designed to be thrown carelessly on the grass. Even the starlings were upset. They flew out over the fjord so that they would not have to watch, they flew right past the swans nesting near the mouth of the river, they flew north in the direction of the Arctic Circle that hovered just on the edge of the horizon.

Ah, but when it was over she was sorry, you want to say, she had learned her lesson, but it was nothing of the sort. It's a curse on the whole family, this inability to feel proper guilt, to learn from our mistakes. We should be wearing sackcoth and ashes, some of us should learn how to pray properly, somebody should ask for forgiveness. But we don't. At least Thorunn didn't. She danced home as happily as if she had won first prize in the confirmation class.

And she did it again. The very next night. She slipped out of doors when she should have been sleeping and lay with Arngrimmur again, just beyond the church in plain view of her father's bedroom, in plain view of her own grandmother's grave. And the next day, when she should have stayed in her room and begged the Lord's forgiveness, she told her sister everything, she told Petrina Soffia who was only fifteen how love happens, the mechanics of the thing. She said it all aloud in the barn when they were feeding the new calf, when anyone might have been listening.

It's a curse on the whole family. We can't keep anything to ourselves. We have to blab it all out, to tell each other things that should never be spoken aloud. We have no secrets, none of us, and no shame. Don't tell us anything, we will tell everyone else, we don't even whisper. You may as well publish your secret in the newspaper as to tell it to us.

And so by the end of the week everyone in the valley knew. Thorunn was so happy about being in love and so amazed with the simple dynamics of lovemaking she told everything to Petrina Soffia. And Petrina was so amazed at her sister's discovery that she told Nanna and Inga, and even their little brother Bjorn, who was only five years old. And Nanna told Disa and Inga told Margaret, and Bjorn thought about it and asked Thorunn, who kissed him and said not to worry, everything would be fine.

That's another problem. We all believe that everything can be cured with kisses. There's no use telling us kisses are part of the problem, that kisses might be the whole problem. We kiss each other when we meet and we kiss each other when we part, and we sometimes kiss perfect strangers. I'll tell you more about that later.

And of course everybody in the valley knew in no time. This is a valley that can't keep secrets. Secrets slide down the slopes of the mountains. Elves whisper the secrets to the cattle. The wind from the fjord blows nobody any good.

So by the time that Arngrimmur's wife found out, Thorunn's belly had begun to swell. The swans on the pond kept their dignity. They nodded their heads and looked at their reflections in the water. The glacier in the south end of the valley moved one more notch toward the fjord. Half the people in the valley packed their bags and moved to America. Arngrimmur bowed his head like a swan and stayed in his house.

Thorunn looked at her reflection in the water and she liked what she saw, the rounding of her belly. She was without shame. When Arngrimmur walked by on the road she waved to him, and she laughed a laugh that haunted him for nine years. He woke in the night in his bed, and the laugh rattled him so he couldn't sleep, and he had to get up in the dark and breathe deeply one hundred times before he could sleep again. For nine whole years.

Did I tell you that we're all plagued by ghosts? Every last one of us, even here in America. It's like this. There were so many ghosts in the valley, there wasn't room for them. And so many people left for America, there was nobody left for the ghosts, so they went to America, too, though not until 1883. One of them is always after me to move his bones. But that comes later. Remind me to tell you about it.

So while Arngrimmur was dealing with that ghost of a laugh, Thorunn's father was making arrangements. He could have sent her to America, but she didn't want to go, and he thought she might get into even more trouble there, in a place that wasn't an island, so you could go anywhere you wanted. And so he married her off to Jon Helgason.

Actually, it wasn't so easy. She didn't want to marry Jon Helgason, even though he had his own farm down the valley, just at the foot of the glacier where the river makes a turn and the bridge keeps falling down. Even though his wife had been dead for ten years, and even though he had his own house and his own sheep and he promised she could have her own horse. Even then she resisted. But then Bjorn drowned in the pond, and everything was too much for a while, and when things settled she was married and had a daughter.

It was a time when children often died, and Thorunn's daughter died, too, even though she did everything she could to keep her alive. It was the whooping cough that took her in the middle of the night, and none of Thorunn's prayers moved God to intervene. Arngrimmur was in sorrow, too, though he couldn't show it. When Thorunn cried at the funeral, her cry entered Arngrimmur's soul, and it haunted him for nine years. Every morning when he awoke, he was so sad he had to take one hundred deep breaths before he could get out of his bed.

Jon Helgason was old, there's no denying that. He was sixty-six when he married Thorunn, and they were married for four years before she shared his bed. Perhaps she was waiting for Arngrimmur, but after a while, there seemed no point in waiting. She had to make the best of things. That's a good thing about us. We all make the best of things. Life isn't always fair, and you have to take what you are given.

Thorunn had two sons with Jon, but they were both albinos with white hair and pink eyes. Jon was so old that his seed had gone bad, and it wasn't strong enough to make a child who could live. Both boys died at the age of two, and Thorunn decided she would have no more children.

But then Arngrimmur's wife died, and he was left alone. His oldest daughter Nanna moved off to America, and the younger children went to live with other people, so he was all by himself. He decided to live his life as a hermit, but he was the only one in the valley who could play the violin, and he was the only one in the valley who could play the flute, and the people needed music, and so even though he was unhappy, he sang and he played, and even though he yearned for Thorunn, and woke in the night to her laugh and in the morning to her cry, he was caught by his life and he had to live it.

And so after a wedding where he had played and sang, he lay in the sweet meadow with another young woman. Only once, he swore, and only half willingly, because she had asked him to. It's a curse on the whole family. We are too polite to refuse, and so rather than hurt anyone's feelings, we populate the planet with the fruits of accidental love. Arngrimmur found himself the father of another daughter. I don't know what became of that daughter. I ought to know. It's written in a book, and I could look it up, but I don't want to. That's a different story, not the story I want to tell.

Here's what happened next. Jon Helgason was climbing onto the back of a horse. He put one foot in the stirrup and swung his leg over the horse. Only he didn't stop. He continued right over the horse onto the ground on the other side, and when Thorunn came to help him up, he was dead.

They buried him right there on the farm, in the exact spot where he had died. And the grass had not even started to grow on his grave before Thorunn married Arngrimmur. Nobody in the valley spoke ill of them for that. Everyone knew they had been meant for each other from the start, and only bad luck had kept them apart. The day they married was nine years after Arngrimmur had heard Thorunn's laugh and his haunting had begun. She laughed again, the night of their wedding, and after that, Arngrimmur slept through the night. She cried the next morning for all their lost children, and Arngrimmur never heard her cry again.

The twentieth century was coming at them like an avalanche and they didn't have much time. They set to work and had four more children. The whole family is like that. When something needs to be done, we get right down to it and do it. Nobody in the valley was happier than Arngrimmur and Thorunn. Once, the new priest preached a sermon which everybody knew was aimed at them. It told a parable about the dangers of lying in the sweet meadows with people who you should not be lying with, but Arngrimmur and Thorunn were so happy that the story ended up with the wrong moral, and the priest never preached it again.

Their children were Nanna and Bjorn and Angantyr and Petrina Soffia, every one of them named for someone else, because that's one way of keeping the dead alive. And after a while Arngrimmur died. I don't like to talk about his death, but I've got a long story to tell and it's best to get the hard parts done early. It was pneumonia. He forgot his coat and walked home without it. A sudden storm brought sleet and rain off the ocean, and Arngrimmur got pneumonia and died.

So this is where the story begins, after Arngrimmur's death when the family had to go and live with relatives and there were twenty-two people living in one house. The story is about the second Petrina Soffia, daughter of Thorunn and Arngrimmur, who was beautiful and good and looked so much like her mother the people in the valley had trouble telling the difference. On her seventeenth birthday, an old farmer down the valley, a nephew of Jon Helgason, offered to marry Petrina Soffia. I told you that there were twenty-two people living in the house, so it was hard for her to refuse.

Petrina Soffia asked her mother what she should do.

Thorunn said only one word.

"America."

And so Petrina Soffia packed up everything she owned, all her clothes and her books, and she put them in her suitcase and she walked all the way to the harbour and boarded a boat and sailed for America. Nobody in Iceland ever heard from her again.

She brought more than her clothes and her books. She brought a memory of mountains and glaciers and fjords. She brought the taste of wild berries on mountain slopes and she carried in her lungs the freshest air in the world. She brought a thousand songs her father had taught her and she brought the memory of how to make ponnokukurs and skyr and how to knit sweaters and how to keep a dying lamb alive. She gathered up all the lonely and abandoned ghosts in Iceland and brought them with her. She brought sweet meadows and the cry of gulls.

And when the boat finally landed in Quebec, she stepped right off into America and into the twentieth century and she never looked back.

Lucky for us.

There Were
Giants, Then

EVERYBODY WAS GOING TO AMERICA. EUROPE HAD CONVULSED and a tide of human bodies rocked their way across the Atlantic. The twentieth century loomed just beyond the horizon, and those who listened carefully could hear its beat, a sort of low intimation of Jazz. Everybody was dressing in blue those days. It was a time for wearing blue.

Arni Peturson was not going to America. America was a place for madmen and fools. He didn't believe in America. When the talk turned to America he started to talk about sheep. He wouldn't listen to any nonsense about ships and rich farmland and opportunities. He would talk about horses instead.

Villingadal is the highest farm in the whole valley. Beyond Villingadal is only lava and snow. The river begins in Villingadal, a spring in the side of the mountain, and by the time it reaches the fjord, it is too wide to cross. What business do Icelanders have in America? Aren't there enough sheep and horses in Iceland without roaming the whole world?

There's a strain of that in the family, a kind of crankiness that won't let us believe anything we haven't seen with our own eyes. Sometimes it can keep you out of trouble, but it can also get you into fights. We're fighters, that's for sure.

The problem was that the bull had gone to America with Thorgeir and his family, and since he had gone, the ice had frozen in the fjord, and for three years in a row there was no summer. The sky filled with ash and darkened, and no grass grew. The sheep died in the fields, and the horses died in the mountains, and the people went to America, and even the ghosts went with them.

Thorgeir's bull had vowed to haunt Thorgeir's family for nine generations, just because Thorgeir's grandfather, Thorgeir the Bald, had given him an indignity. That Thorgeir had gone in to have supper when the bull was only half-skinned after he had killed it. It was a stupid thing to do. Anyone knows that if you don't finish skinning an animal, it will come back and haunt you.

And now Thorgeir Thorgeirsson, son of Thorgeir Thorgeirsson the Bald, son of Thorgeir Thorgeirsson the Strong, had gone to America and the bull had gone with him. The bull had been a nuisance, trampling the rhubarb at night, coming as a barking dog and frightening the sheep, bellowing in the high passes until finally the wind joined him in his howling, and storms made the river flood, even right there in the valley where it began. But the bull kept the other ghosts under control, and Arni missed it.

Did I tell you that on that side we are descended from giants? Arni Peturson was two full metres in height and all his sons and daughters were taller than him. They were the finest Glima wrestlers in all of Eyafjorthur. All four of the boys could beat anyone but his own brothers, and each of the three girls could beat any man in the district.

The famous Lifting Rock was right there in Villingadal, just south of the barn. Arni Peturson had lifted it, and his father, Petur Arnason, had lifted it as had his father Arni Peturson, and so on back to the giants who had first put it there when the world began. All the sons could lift the rock and so could all the daughters, but there was no other man in the north of Iceland who could budge it. The girls had vowed they would marry no man who could not lift the rock, and so Margaret had to wait until Sveinn Bjornson came from Reykjavik and lifted it, and Helga had to wait until Grimsi Magnusson came from the east and lifted it, and Disa would never have married at all if a Norwegian named Bjorn hadn't come and lifted it when Disa was forty years old, and nearly past child-bearing. But that's a different story. I'll tell it to you another time.

It's Johann I want to tell you about, and the courting of Dorothea Soffia Abrahamsdottir. Here's what happened. When Johann was seventeen years old, he went to a tombola at Grund on the other side of the river. His mother wanted to go, because her sister Rosa was going to be there, and Arni told Johann to take her, because there was haying to do, and the sun had finally come out after forty days of rain.

Johann did not want to go when there was work to be done, but he saddled up two horses and he and his mother rode for four hours along the path to the bridge across the river. Then they rode four hours back along the other side of the river until they came to Grund. The tombola was just as boring as Johann had thought it would be. But just as his mother was saying goodbye to her sister Rosa, Dorothea Soffia Abrahamsdottir walked into the room. She had long black hair and hazel eyes. Johann heard a loud crack, like the sound of thunder or the crack of an earthquake, and he realized that it was his heart that had made the noise. Dorothea smiled at him, and he felt as if his insides had turned to liquid. Then he ran out of the room, harnessed the horses, and gathered up his mother to take her home.

It was too late. He was hooked so solidly into love that there was no chance that he could ever be free again. All the way to the bridge he cursed his fate, and swore that he would never be made a slave, but his heart was paying no attention to him. It had begun singing, and Dorothea's image was imprinted on the inside of his eyelids, so that even if he closed his eyes, he still saw her.

Johann's mother told him to forget about her. Dorothea was the daughter of Abraham Hallgrimsson from Hildihargi, the richest man in Eyafjorthur, and his wife Frithrika, who was famous for her beauty. She was descended from Norwegian kings. She would not marry Johann Arnason, the son of Arni Peturson, who didn't even believe in America.

Johann agreed with his mother. He knew that there was no chance in the world that Dorothea had even noticed him or that even if she did notice him, she would marry him. But that didn't stop him from dreaming of her all that night and all the next night, too. It didn't stop him from thinking of her all day long and it didn't stop his heart from singing its own maddening song.

Then one week later, just at dusk, Johann looked up from the stones he was piling for a fence and he saw a figure in a black robe on the top of the cliff on the other side of the river. He knew immediately it was Dorothea. Nobody had ever appeared at the edge of that cliff before, and Johann knew what it meant.

He ran to the stone bridge that crossed the river down by the waterfall. It was the only way across the river unless you harnessed a horse and rode for two hours. The trouble was that the cliff was twenty metres high, and it was perfectly vertical. There was barely a foothold anywhere, but that didn't bother Johann. He clambered up the cliff as if he were a goat. He forgot that he was two metres tall and that he weighed a hundred kilos and that he would be a certain corpse if he fell. It was pitch dark when he reached the top, and Dorothea was nowhere to be seen.

He shouted her name, but she did not answer. Then he caught a whiff of her perfume on the air, and he followed that smell for a mile until he came to a mighty farm with a dozen barns. The farmhouse had glass windows, something that Johann had heard about but had never seen before. Through the windows, the light of lamps poured out onto the ground, and inside, he could see a figure in a black robe.

He was looking through the window when the men of Hildihargi jumped on him. Eight men grabbed at him and struck at him. They called him a dog, and swore that he would regret that he had come onto the land of his betters. It was a mighty battle but when it was over, Johann had stacked all eight of the men in a pile and knocked at the door. A man in rich clothes answered the door and asked him what he wanted. He said he wanted to speak with Dorothea, and gave his name.

"You are the son of Arni Peturson?"

"Yes."

"I am Abraham Hallgrimsson. Let me shake your hand."

Johann gave Abraham his hand, and Abraham squeezed his hand harder than any man had ever squeezed it before. Johann returned the squeeze, and the two men stood there locked together until finally Abraham relented and called Dorothea.

She was even more beautiful than he had remembered, and Johann suddenly felt himself gross and clumsy. His legs were the thickness of tree trunks, his chest like a barrel, his head a block of wood thatched with yellow straw, his eyes a no-colour blue, and she was delicate and dark.

"May I call on you?" he asked.

"You may come on Sunday," she said. "I will see you at the church."

"I will come Sunday at afternoon coffee," he told her. "I will not enter a church."

"You will not be welcome then," she said.

"We'll see," he answered, and he walked back out the door. The men had unstacked themselves, and were moaning and cursing, but they did not try their luck with Johann again.

Somehow, he climbed back down the cliff and made his way home. His father was waiting for him.

"Is it a sacrilege to enter a church if you do not believe?" Johann asked him.

"You may enter for weddings and funerals," his father said. "But if you enter for any other reason, then you are a hypocrite."

Johann said nothing, but he sat outside in the damp night for hours, trying to ponder out what he must do. He could not marry a wife who would insist he go to church, and if he did not go to church, it appeared that Dorothea would not be his wife.

The next night was Friday, but he scaled the cliff anyway and made his way to Abraham's farm. This time he did not go close, but only sat on a rock and watched the farm until dawn. Then he climbed back down the cliff and went home.

The third night he sat on the fence near one of the barns. The lights were out in the house, and Johann stared so hard in his desire to see Dorothea that he nearly lighted up the house by the heat of his gaze. Then, without warning, his eyes were covered by soft hands, and a sweet voice whispered his name.

"Will you marry me?" he asked.

"Yes," she said. "I will marry you somehow, though it will have to be without my father's permission if you cannot go to church."

"I cannot do it."

"Then we'd better get busy," she said. "If we are going to marry without a church, there is no need to wait." And she led him to the barn, and there in the barn was the making of Frithrika Johannsdottir begun.

Afterwards, they walked together to the cliff.

"What do we do now?" Johann asked.

Dorothea looked deep into his lake-blue eyes.

"America," she said, and she kissed him again.

Then the waves of the Atlantic began to fret, and storms hurried down from the north. All the birds in Iceland rose up in protest, and cried out their dismay. But the St. Lawrence River swelled and America opened its arms and prepared to receive them, and there was nothing left that anyone could do.

The Wizard
of the Westman

We don't always tell this story, because people don't like to know you are descended from wizards. But this is how it goes.

A LONG TIME AGO, WHEN THE BLACK DEATH WAS RAVAGING Iceland, eighteen wizards gathered in a group and moved to the Westman Islands so that they could escape death for as long as possible. For a long time, they didn't know whether anyone on the mainland had survived, but as summer turned to fall and winter approached, they decided they would have to know whether it was safe to return, so they sent one of their group over to investigate. The man they sent was neither the greatest wizard nor was he the least. His name was Tomas, and he was exactly the average of the group. They took him across the water, and dropped him off on the shore of Iceland, telling him that if he were not back by Christmas, they would dispatch a sending, an evil ghost raised from the dead to kill him. Tomas knew the other wizards' powers, and he did not dispute what they said.

He set off to find what he could and for a long time he

ranged the coast of Iceland, but he found no one alive. The doors of all the houses were open, and bodies lay wherever they had fallen, fathers and mothers and children. Finally, just as he was about to give up his quest, he arrived at a farm where the door was shut. He knocked at the door and a beautiful young woman answered it.

When she saw him, she threw herself into his arms weeping with joy to see another human, because she thought she was the only survivor in all of Iceland. She said that her name was Soffia. She begged the wizard to stay with her, and because he was smitten with her beauty, he agreed to stay for a short while. He told her though that he would have to go back to the Westman Islands before Christmas.

They talked for hours. She told him she had travelled for a week in every direction without meeting a living soul, and that she had faced the horror of seeing all her friends and relatives dead. He told her about the eighteen wizards and their pact, and about his own dismal journey. They were full of stories and they told them to each other through the days and nights.

For a while they were happy, but inevitably Christmas arrived. Soffia begged the wizard to stay with her. She told him that his fellows could not be so cruel as to kill him for helping a poor orphan. Poor Tomas couldn't decide whether to stay or to go. Then, when Christmas Eve arrived, he decided that he would have to return. For a long time Soffia pleaded with him, and they held each other and wept at the cruel fate that would separate them. Then, just as the sun began to set, she changed her plea.

"Do you think you can reach the islands tonight?" She asked him. "Isn't it better to die here in my arms insted of in a lonesome ship on the sea?" Tomas realized Soffia had detained him until his death was inevitable, but he had fallen so in love that he would sooner die with her than live alone, and he agreed to stay.

The night wore on, and the young wizard became increasingly despondent. The girl, however, was as cheerful as could be, and she asked him how the other wizards were getting on. He told her that they had already dispatched the sending, and the ghost would arrive that very night. The girl sat on the bed with the wizard, and he lay against the wall. He was getting increasingly drowsy, which he blamed on the sending, and he soon fell asleep. His arms and legs began to feel as if he were already in his grave. The girl shook him awake, and he told her that the sending was now on the very farm, and he fell into such a deep sleep that he couldn't be awakened.

Soffia sat on the edge of the bed, and she watched the door. Soon a rust-coloured vapour began to seep under the door. It welled up before her and took on a human shape. The girl asked it where it thought it was going, and the sending explained that it had come to kill the wizard, so if she would just move out of its way, he would do the job and get back to his grave.

Soffia said that she would be glad to move, but only if the sending did her a favour. She had never met a sending before, and she was curious about his powers. The sending seemed pleased that someone was interested in him, and he asked her what she wanted.

"Can you make yourself as large as you can?" she asked. The sending puffed itself up until it filled the whole house.

"And now can you make yourself as small as you can?"

The sending immediately turned itself into a fly. It tried to sneak under the girl's arm to get to Tomas on the bed, but the girl caught it in a hollow sheep's bone and popped in a plug. A few minutes later, Tomas awoke and could hardly believe he was alive.

"This is just as I thought," Soffia said. "Those wizards on the Westman Islands are not as smart as they think they are."

Then they celebrated Christmas with skyr and ponnokokkurs and kleinur and svid. They drank many cups of coffee with good heavy cream and they sucked the coffee through lumps of sugar, but as New Year's drew near, Tomas again became silent. Soffia asked him what was bothering him, and he told her he feared that they had sent another sending, and this one was more powerful than the last. It would not be so easily tricked.

Soffia just laughed and told him not to worry. She was so cheerful that the wizard was ashamed of his fear, and he joined her in celebrating the New Year.

But the sun went behind the clouds and the winds started to roar, and soon Tomas could sense that the second sending had arrived at the farm. He told Soffia, and she led him to a small birch forest not far from the house. There, she lifted a flat stone, and led him into a cave. It was dark and terrifying inside the cave. The cave was lit by a dim lamp made out of a human skull and inside it burned the belly fat of a man. An ancient man with bloodshot eyes and a long grey beard sat there.

"Are you there, Foster Father?" Soffia asked.

"Something terrible must be happening, Foster Daughter," the man said to the girl. "It's a long time since I've seen you. What can I do for you?"

The girl told the man the whole story of the wizard and the ghosts and she gave him the sending she had captured in the hollow sheep's bone.

"I hope you can help us, Foster Father," she said, "for Tomas is becoming drowsy, and that's a sure sign of a sending."

The old man opened the sheep's bone and released the fly. He caressed and patted it, and said, "Now go and meet all the sendings from the Westman Islands and swallow them all up."

Then the fly grew so large that one of its jaws touched the sky and the other scraped the earth. It flew off to the Westman Islands, and it ate up all the sendings it found there. Then Tomas and Soffia returned to the farm, and there they settled down and married and multiplied and filled the earth that had been emptied by the Black Death. And that's why we're here today.